THE ADVENTURERS AND
THE TEMPLE OF TREASURE

By Jemma Hatt

The Adventurers and the Temple of Treasure

Copyright © 2019 to Jemma Hatt

www.jemmahatt.com

This is a work of fiction. Although actual places are used in some cases, all characters and happenings are fabricated.

Editing by Amanda: www.letsgetbooked.com

Cover Illustration by Andrew Smith:
www.andrewsmithartist.myportfolio.com

ISBN: 978-1-9993641-1-3

Other Books in
The Adventurers Series

For Dawn

Table of Contents

Chapter 1
Tom Arrives

The idea of London train travel is often so much nicer than the reality. Shuffling onto the Underground with too much to carry, wedged between a tall man's armpit and someone else's rucksack pressed into your chest, does not exactly allow for a comfortable experience. Especially whilst trying not to think about the jumble of smells attacking your nostrils from every direction and the spilt drink on the floor edging closer and closer towards your trainers.

The challenges of the Tube were heightened by the three cake tins Tom's mother had given him to balance alongside his luggage. Nevertheless, his spirits were high. It was his first time outside Cornwall and he was going to spend the October half term with his best friends: Lara, Rufus and their dog Barney. No amount of body odour, bad-tempered commuters or confusing station layouts was going to bring him down.

At long last, Tom struggled his way into Charing Cross Station and heaved his suitcase and cake tins onto a train heading towards Swindlebrook. As he took his mobile phone out of his pocket (his thirteenth birthday present from his parents and Great Uncle Herb) a flurry of messages and missed calls greeted him.

How are you getting on? Hope the cakes haven't been squished. Love Mum xx (Mrs Burt always closed her text messages as if they were letters).

Are you on the train to Swindlebrook yet? Love Mum xx

Tom, you're not picking up my calls. Are you alright? Love Mum xx

Hello? Love Mum xx

THOMAS BURT! RING ME IMMEDIATELY! Love Mum xx

Tom hastily texted a reply to his mother and leant back in his seat, watching the scenery out of the window as the tower blocks and busy streets gave way to fields and villages. At Swindlebrook Station's exit, he was greeted by a welcoming sight: Rufus Kexley, his cousin Lara Jacobs and Lara's dog, Barney. As soon as Tom made his way through the barrier Barney flung himself at him, sending the cake tins flying. Rufus deftly caught them.

"Mrs B, she never disappoints," said Rufus, already unwrapping a cupcake from one of the tins.

"Can't you wait until we've got home, greedy guts," scolded Lara as she rolled her eyes. "Hi, Tom! Mum's in the car."

The cousins led Tom – who was holding Barney in his arms and being coated in licks – to the car.

"Hello Tom," said Mrs Jacobs, flicking her long black hair away from her face as she buckled up. "How was the train— *Rufus!* We're having our dinner before you scoff any more of those cakes."

Rufus put one of the cupcakes back into the tin and slid another into his coat pocket.

To Tom, the small red brick detached house surrounded by other identical houses felt a million miles away from the run-down castle where he lived with his parents and Great Uncle Herb. During the summer holidays, when he met Rufus and Lara for the first time, they had stumbled upon a treasure hunt and discovered hidden Egyptian treasure. It was hard to imagine such an adventure happening in the neat and smart countryside town of Swindlebrook, but Tom was thrilled simply to be with his friends.

Whilst eating their spaghetti, the phone rang, and Mrs Jacobs went to answer it. A few minutes later, Rufus was getting restless.

"We might as well crack open the chocolate cake," he said, looking longingly at one of Mrs Burt's cake tins on the worktop.

"Wait till Mum gets back," said Lara, "she hasn't finished her dinner yet."

Rufus sighed heavily. Twenty minutes passed as Lara and Tom chatted about school and Cornwall, whilst Rufus fidgeted in his seat and rubbed his skinny belly.

"I can't wait anymore!" he cried, jumping up and snatching the cake tin. At that moment, Mrs Jacobs re-entered the room with a tired expression.

"Well, we've got another visitor coming tomorrow," she said with a faint smile.

"Who?" asked Lara, as Rufus stealthily slid the cake tin away from him on the worktop and casually sat back down at the table.

"Uncle Logan; he's your dad's younger brother."

"I thought he was abroad doing some TV show?" asked Lara.

"His show stopped a couple of years ago," Mrs Jacobs replied. "He was filming by the Amazon river and something happened … I'm not sure what …"

"Wait …" said Tom, his eyes flashing in recognition. "Your uncle is Logan Jacobs? As in *Logan's Jungle Trek*? I used to watch that show!"

"Where's he going to sleep? He can't have my room, I've got too much stuff," said Rufus, thinking of the hoard of practical joke supplies and props stashed around his bedroom.

"He can have the spare room. Tom, we'll set up the camp bed for you in Rufus' room."

Mrs Jacobs cleared away the plates, and to Rufus' infinite relief, picked up the cake tin. At that moment, the telephone rang again, and she walked into the hallway to answer it, absent-mindedly carrying the cake with her.

"Shuzbucket!" snapped Rufus, banging his fist on the table. He followed his aunt out of the room determined to bring back the cake.

"What's Logan like?" Tom asked Lara.

"I don't really remember him much," she replied. "Last time he was here I was only four or five, we went to the local fairground."

"This is how it all started in the summer," said Tom, stroking his chin, "with an uncle you didn't really know."

"It started before then," said Lara, smiling at the memory of their summer adventure. "Mum was called away abroad for work."

Rufus re-entered the room and slammed the door shut behind him with a bang.

"You'll never guess!" he cried, clutching the table. "Someone from your mum's work is on the phone; she's been called away to Egypt!"

Chapter 2
An Arrival and a Departure

The following day, the house was in turmoil. Logan was supposed to arrive at nine o'clock in the morning so that his sister-in-law could spend a few hours issuing detailed instructions on looking after Lara, Rufus, Tom and Barney, before leaving for the airport at one o'clock. It was now a quarter past one and there was still no sign of him. Mrs Jacobs had called the number she had saved in her mobile phone for Logan several times, without success. She was pacing up and down, her suitcase by the front door. Lara and Tom, sitting on the stairs, felt quite sorry for Lara's worried mother. Even Rufus, who was keeping watch from the kitchen window, was starting to feel a pang of sympathy.

"I'll have to cancel my trip," said Mrs Jacobs. "I can't *believe* he would do this to me. When I called him back last night, he swore he would be able to come early and look after you all."

"You can't cancel the trip," said Lara, "you worked too hard on the excavation."

"I know … they'll cancel the funding for the whole project now since I can't make the meetings," said Mrs Jacobs, looking up at the ceiling with a sigh.

"Sorry Mrs Jacobs," said Tom. "Is there anything we can do?"

"No … thank you, Tom. I'll call my supervisor now."

Lara and Tom moved out of the way as Mrs Jacobs made her way upstairs.

"Why don't we get out of here," said Lara. "My friend Daisy lives across the street."

Lara and Tom called Rufus and they walked out of the front door with Barney. Suddenly they stopped at the pavement, hearing a rumbling sound in the distance.

"Can you hear that?" asked Lara.

"It's getting louder," said Tom.

A roaring Jeep spun around the corner, startling a middle-aged couple on the pavement within an inch of their lives. Barney barked excitedly as Lara held his collar to stop him running into the street. The vehicle barrelled towards them, screeching to a halt with a deafening engine backfire.

A man jumped out of the car looking panicked. He was tall and tanned with muscular arms and short black hair; wearing a beige cargo shirt and brown shorts.

"You must be the kids," he said, his eyes wide with alarm. "I'm your uncle, Logan. Where's your mum, did she leave for the airport?" he asked, looking around.

"No, she was waiting for you!" cried Lara.

"Oh, cripes," said Logan, charging into the house at top speed.

"That's one way to make an entrance," observed Rufus.

"What's going to happen now?" Lara wondered out loud. "Mum won't like him turning up hours late like this without calling."

Lara's question was shortly answered as the door flung open and Uncle Logan was guiding Mrs Jacobs out with one hand and hauling her large suitcase in the other. The three watched with equal fascination and surprise.

"I really can't leave things like this, we've hardly had a chance to say two words to each other," protested Mrs Jacobs.

"It will all be fine, Sarah, trust me."

"Why wasn't your phone ringing when I called you?"

"It got disconnected this morning, *slight* billing issue," Logan said, pressing his thumb and forefinger together.

"I'll get it all sorted out tonight, before your flight even lands. Trust me."

Logan had somehow managed to get hold of Mrs Jacobs' car keys and was squeezing her case into the boot.

"Will you *stop* telling me to trust you. How can I trust you with the children when you can't even pay your phone bill?"

Logan had finally managed to fit the suitcase into the boot and slammed down the hood. He turned to Mrs Jacobs and put a hand on her shoulder.

"Sarah, I know I've screwed things up in the past, but I swear to you, I will *not* screw this up. The kids are staying in their own house, we'll be fine. Won't we, kids?"

Both Logan and Mrs Jacobs turned to face Lara, Rufus and Tom.

"Err, yeah," said Lara, fidgeting with her long dark hair.

"Sure," said Tom, staring at the floor.

"Absolutely," said Rufus, grinning from ear to ear. For Rufus, the best kinds of adults were the ones who had no control over any given situation. First impressions indicated that Logan would not disappoint.

"See," said Logan. "We're all good. Now get yourself out of here Sarah, you're running *so* late for your flight."

Mrs Jacobs shot a thunderous glance at Logan before walking over to the kids. "Are you sure you'll be alright?" she asked.

"You should go, Mum," said Lara. "You can call us at the other end and Daisy's parents are just over the road."

Tom smiled encouragingly. Rufus, concerned that his aunt would either change her mind or stall for too long and miss her flight, quickly pulled everyone into a group hug.

"Bye, Auntie Sarah!" he yelled, before running over to open the car door.

Mrs Jacobs, still looking uncertain, moved into the driver's seat.

"Logan, I've left some money and a credit card in the bedside drawer in your room," she said.

"Awesome," said Logan, his eyes lighting up in glee, before composing himself. "Err, I mean, okay, thanks."

"If *anything* happens, call me immediately."

"Right-ho."

"Bye," shouted Mrs Jacobs to the children. "Speak to you later tonight."

"Bye," called Logan, Tom, Lara and Rufus in unison. Mrs Jacobs pulled the car out of the driveway and soon disappeared around the corner.

Chapter 3
The Watch

Logan turned to Lara, Rufus and Tom after Mrs Jacobs had left.

"So … which one of you am I related to?" he asked, scratching his head.

"You don't even *know*?" said Lara, scrunching her face into her best look of disgust, which was usually reserved for Rufus after one of his pranks.

"Oh yeah … it's you, Clara … of *course* I knew it was you."

"Lara!"

"Lara, yeah, that's what I meant. How about you boys?"

Tom introduced himself quietly and shook hands with Logan. Lara introduced Barney who held a paw politely to Logan, who took it and patted his head.

"And you?" Logan asked, glancing back at Rufus.

"I'm Joe," Rufus replied. "Joe King."

"Hi Joe," said Logan. Tom and Lara struggled to hide their snorts of laughter. "Right, do me a favour kids and take my stuff into my room, would you? I'm starving, let's see what there is in the kitchen …"

Logan walked back into the house.

"Not very bright, is he?" said Rufus.

"No, he's not, *Joe*!" laughed Tom.

"*And* he's lazy," complained Lara. "I can't believe he's left us out here with his boxes while he's stuffing his face with our food already."

They looked up to the kitchen window to see Logan happily taking a huge bite out of leftover pizza from three days ago. He looked up, grinned and waved.

"*I* was saving that," said Rufus, through gritted teeth as he waved back at Logan. "Well, he's made his first two big mistakes. Eating my pizza … and leaving us alone with all his stuff."

"Joe King by name, jo-king by nature, eh," said Tom. They turned to the Jeep and started to lift out the raggedy cardboard boxes that held Logan's belongings.

"Is *that* your uncle?"

The three looked up to see Lara's friend Daisy Duncely crossing the street.

"Unfortunately," said Lara.

"Oh … my …" said Daisy, twirling strands of her hair between her fingers. "I saw him when his car pulled up. He's so …"

"Stupid," said Rufus.

"Greedy," added Tom.

"Vain," said Lara, staring at the window.

The others looked back towards the kitchen to see that Logan had finished demolishing the pizza slice and was inspecting and tweaking his hair using the reflection from the microwave door. He glanced outside and gave another friendly smile and wave.

"Dreamy," gasped Daisy, placing both hands on her chest. "Wasn't he on that TV show? Wait till I tell my sister about *this*."

"Ewww," said Rufus, his face twisting in revulsion. "You can't *like* Logan!"

"Nobody could, after they've met him," said Lara with her arms folded.

"I can't meet him?" said Daisy, horror-struck at the thought. "What would I say to him? What would I do? It would be *so* awkward!" She covered her face with her hands.

"Why are you being so weird?" asked Lara. "He's boring and lazy."

"I need to plan what I'm going to say," said Daisy.

"You've never had that trouble before," said Lara. It was true; Daisy was a natural chatterbox and was always being told by her teachers to stop gossiping and passing notes in class.

"I need time," cried Daisy.

"Looks like you're out of time," said Tom. At that moment Logan was opening the front door again, holding a multi-pack of crisps.

"Hurry up with those boxes, kids," he yelled, tearing open the bag and pulling out three packets. "I need to move the Jeep into the garage before it rains."

"Fine! Daisy will you help us carry these—" Lara turned around but only caught the back of Daisy's head in sight as her friend sprinted back into her garden through the back gate.

"Who's that? Another relation?"

"*No,*" snapped Lara. Logan shrugged and returned to the kitchen with his crisps.

Half an hour later, Tom and Lara heaved the last of Logan's boxes to Mrs Jacobs' room, where Logan would be staying. They sat down on the floor, panting.

"Why does he have so much stuff just for a few weeks?" asked Tom.

"I was wondering that too," said Lara. "Oh no …" she clapped her hands against her forehead. "His TV show got cancelled and he doesn't have another one ... he couldn't pay his phone bill ... his car is so banged up it sounds like it's about to explode ..."

"He's homeless," said Tom, finishing her train of thought. "He might be here a while, you know."

Lara groaned.

Rufus came up the stairs and flopped next to the boxes. "Logan's using the phone downstairs, check this out," he said, picking up the landline phone in Mrs Jacobs' room and turning on the speaker.

"Dee ... I know I messed up, I'm sorry," they heard Logan say through the telephone downstairs in the hall. "Just give me one more chance?"

"Logan, it's been two years, I've *moved on*," said Dee.

"But please... I miss you so much."

"Well, you should have thought about that before you disappeared off travelling without telling me. I deserve better."

"I know you do, Dee, but I'm a changed man. Give me a chance."

Lara clicked the phone off.

"He's even more of a loser than I thought," she scorned.

"There's *so* much junk," said Rufus, who had placed a safari hat on his head as he rummaged through Logan's belongings. He flung a didgeridoo, a straggly piece of rope and pair of miniature bongo drums on the floor. Barney eagerly picked up the wooden didgeridoo and carried it to Lara's feet.

"That's not a stick Barney," she laughed, as the dog wagged his tail excitedly.

"Look at *this*," Rufus yelled, holding up an old watch with a leather strap.

"Where did you get that from?" asked Lara, her face suddenly turning pale. She had seen the watch before.

"From this shoebox," said Rufus, throwing it at his cousin. Papers and photographs fell out onto the floor and Lara rushed to pick them up.

"*Lucas*," said Tom, reading the messy handwriting scrawled across the front of the box. "Who's that, Lara?"

Lara hesitated a moment before answering.

"My dad," she said.

Chapter 4
Lucas

Rufus and Tom were quiet as Lara picked up the photographs, including one of a tall, dark-haired man wearing the watch on his wrist as he stood outside a tent in the desert. They knew that Lara's father had died when she was a baby, in Egypt, where he had worked on archaeological digs alongside her mother.

"Mum has got most of these photos as well," said Lara, smiling at a photograph of her parents together on a riverboat.

At that moment, footsteps came up the stairs.

"Why are you guys taking so long … hey Joe, take that off." Logan pulled the safari hat off Rufus' head. He noticed that Barney was holding the large didgeridoo in his mouth. "That is *not* a toy," he yelled, trying to swipe the musical instrument and tripping over the dog instead.

"Uncle Logan … why have you got so much of my dad's stuff?" asked Lara.

"Wha…what?" Logan looked confused and then noticed the photographs, papers and envelopes on the floor. "Who said you guys could go through my things? Your dad sent me a load of stuff for safekeeping while he was in Egypt. Every now and then he'd send me another envelope and I'd put it in a box. When he passed … your mum gave me his watch. It was our dad's before he gave it to Lucas."

Lara started to gather all of the envelopes from the floor.

"You haven't even opened most of these," she said, her face flushing pink. "They must be important for him to have sent them to you."

"Well, I didn't get rid of them, did I?" said Logan, shuffling uncomfortably. "To tell you the truth, I opened a couple and couldn't make neither head nor tail of them. They were in all different languages. I didn't like to bother your mother with it, especially at that time – she was going through enough as it was."

Lara tore open the letters one by one and quickly scanned the contents.

"They're in Arabic mostly …" she said, "and there's some hieroglyphics here." She pointed to the page.

"Hiero-what?" Logan looked blank.

"It's the ancient Egyptian style of writing, using pictures and symbols."

"Can you read it?" Tom asked.

"No … but there are a few symbols I can make out," said Lara, tracing the drawings with her fingertips. "Spirits … afterlife … riches …"

"Riches?" Rufus piped up.

"We need to take this to someone who can translate the symbols," said Lara.

"Who?" asked Logan.

"I know just the person who can help," Lara replied with a smile.

Chapter 5
A Reunion

The next morning, Logan, Lara, Tom, Rufus and Barney were standing on the pavement outside a block of apartments in East London. Logan had driven there in his Jeep, which was still making an alarming set of engine noises.

"How did you get his address?" Rufus asked Lara.

"It was in Mum's address book in the kitchen."

The front door buzzed, and they let themselves into the bare hallway and walked up the steps to the top floor. A young man wearing a pair of smart jeans and a shirt was holding the door open for them.

"Hi Karim," said Lara.

"Hey guys," greeted Karim with a warm smile. He patted Barney and led the group into a small living room. Logan sat in an armchair and Lara, Tom and Rufus squeezed onto a small sofa. Barney rolled onto his back as Lara stroked his black, white and tan fur with her foot.

"Let me make you something to drink," said Karim, "my little sister sent me some chamomile tea from Cairo – want to try it?"

Everyone thanked Karim, and he went into the kitchen to boil the kettle.

"How do you know Karim again?" asked Logan.

"During the summer we found treasure hidden near the castle where I live," said Tom proudly. "Karim saved our lives when we were trapped by the tides on the beach."

Karim shortly returned with mugs on a tray and Logan helped him pass them around.

"Here you go, Joe," said Logan, handing a mug to Rufus. Karim shot Logan a confused look.

"How is your mother?" he asked Lara. "Wonderful woman, I've enjoyed working with her at the university."

"She's okay," said Lara, "she had to go back to Alexandria yesterday for a meeting with some people who are paying for an Egyptian excavation project. She should be back in a few days though."

"And what is it I can help you with?"

Lara took her father's documents from her backpack, clipped together in date order. Karim carefully read each one slowly. Every now and then he made an 'aha' or 'hmm' sound, without remarking on the contents. Rufus drummed his feet on the floor in anticipation and tapped the side of the sofa with his hands. At long last, Karim cleared his throat to speak.

"Your father was onto something here," he said to Lara. Everyone automatically leaned forward in their seats. Even Barney pricked up his ears. "The letters in Arabic are from a man named Abdul, to your father. He's discussing the discovery at the Royal Cache."

"Royal what?" Rufus interrupted.

"That's where all those mummies were found, isn't it?" asked Lara.

"Yes," Karim continued. "The royal tombs were being opened and looted by tomb robbers for treasure. A group of priests hid the bodies of over fifty ancient royals together to keep them safe for eternity."

"What about the treasure?" asked Rufus, his eyes wide.

"Well ..." said Karim, "it was always assumed that the treasure had already been taken, or that the priests stole the treasure and kept it for themselves. However ..." He flicked back to one of the pages.

"However?" repeated Logan, who was becoming as fidgety as Rufus.

"This friend of Mr Jacobs, Abdul, well he seems to think the priests hid the treasure *somewhere else.*"

There was a series of gasps in the room. Both Lara and Tom felt goose bumps on their arms and legs.

"It's happening again," Tom said to Lara quietly. "Another adventure." They both smiled.

"Why would they do that?" Logan asked Karim.

"Well, he doesn't say," said Karim, resting his hand on his chin. "But I can think of one reason. They wanted to keep both the treasure and the mummies safe – but above all, the mummies. By keeping the treasure separate, if the mummies were found they wouldn't interest common tomb robbers."

"Because of the lack of gold?" added Tom.

"Exactly. And if the robbers were convinced that there wasn't any treasure, they wouldn't disturb the mummies while looking for it."

"Does Abdul say where to find the gold?" yelled Rufus, jumping out of his seat as if he were about to start the search immediately.

"Well … no," Karim answered with a frown. "There are a few hieroglyphics that suggest the treasure is in a hidden temple … but there are so many temples in Egypt, who knows which one it could be?"

"There must be a reason Dad kept all those letters and drawings," said Lara. "Is there an address for Abdul?"

"No … but the letters mention that he works at the Egyptian Museum. Obviously, this was a while ago, you're mentioned as a one-year-old in one of these letters."

"Eleven years ago." Lara cast her eyes to the floor. "It must have been right before he died."

"What's Abdul's last name?" asked Tom.

"Faruk. Dr Abdul Faruk."

Tom took his phone from his pocket and typed in the name.

"He's still there," he said, showing his phone to Lara. "Antiquities specialist."

"I wish I had a phone," whined Rufus.

"Me too," added Logan.

"You've got one!" cried Lara. "Get it reactivated, Mum might be trying to call you."

Logan mentally made a note to borrow from his sister-in-law's credit card to settle his phone bill.

"Call Abdul at the museum, Tom," shouted Rufus. "Do it now, pleeaaase!"

"There's no number here," said Tom. "And my mum will go nuts if I get a phone bill with long-distance calls."

"I'll try," said Karim. "I should have a number somewhere for the museum …"

Karim took his phone from the coffee table and found the number to call. He proceeded to have a conversation in Arabic lasting several minutes. At times, he raised his voice and became quite animated, then finally ended the call, looking downcast.

"I finally got through to Dr Abdul," he explained. "He became very defensive when I mentioned Lucas Jacobs. He said he would not enter into any conversation on the subject by telephone or email. I thought he sounded very suspicious. I'm sorry … I couldn't get any information from him."

Lara and Tom sighed whilst Rufus slammed his fist on the arm of the sofa. Only Logan looked unperturbed.

"There's only one thing for it then," he said. "We're going to Egypt."

Chapter 6
Dee

Before leaving Karim's apartment, Lara, Rufus and Tom tried to persuade their friend to join them on their trip.

"I wish I could," Karim said with wistful eyes, "but I have to stay in London. My visa is being renewed and I can't travel anywhere. Otherwise, I would have covered the meetings for Mrs Jacobs in Alexandria this week. But I'll give you the address of my family in Cairo – if you ever need anything, they'll be sure to help you out. My little sister Maye is eleven, Rufus' age."

"Rufus? Oh, you mean Joe," said Logan. Karim smiled, but said nothing.

They left Karim's apartment shortly after and piled back into the Jeep. Rufus sat in the front, and Barney sat between Lara and Tom in the back. As the car wheezed and spluttered down the road, Lara wondered whether Logan's plan was realistic.

"How are we all going to get to Egypt?" she asked. "We can't leave Barney."

Barney woofed in agreement.

"What about that kid who lives opposite you?" suggested Logan, swerving the car dangerously as he looked behind him.

"Watch the *road*," warned Lara. "*Daisy Duncely*? I can't leave Barney with her. She can't even keep plants alive. She killed our form's cactus when she took it home from school."

Logan hummed. "Well I think I know someone who might be able to help," he said. "That's if she'll talk to me this time…"

About an hour later Logan pressed a buzzer next to a pair of tall, black iron gates.

"Logan!" screeched the metal speaker, as Logan jumped back in surprise.

"Dee! How'd you know it was me?"

"I can see you through the security camera, you dummy."

Logan instinctively adjusted his hair in the Jeep's wing mirror and waved up at the camera fixed to the top of the gate. Lara and Tom cringed, while Rufus shook his head.

"Still conceited as ever, I see," snapped Dee.

"Let me in, Dee," whined Logan.

"No!"

"Please?"

"Go *away*."

Logan sighed and was about to return to the car when he remembered his four passengers.

"Let us in, I've got three kids with me," he pleaded.

Barney howled.

"And a Border collie," Logan added.

"How dare you use them to worm your way in?"

"I'm not … but please let us in."

A few moments of silence passed. Tom, Rufus and Lara smiled meekly up towards the camera. Barney threw his head back and howled even louder.

"Blast you, Logan."

A buzzing noise was followed by the gates swinging open. Logan jumped back into the car, banging his knee against the steering wheel. He yelled out in pain as laughter rang out from the speaker.

Logan drove up a long drive towards a large brick mansion with several outbuildings. At the front door was a tall, slim woman in her late twenties with long thick black curly hair. She was wearing a sweater, cargo pants and hiking boots.

Barney took an instant liking to Dee and pelted towards her, jumping and licking her hands as she laughed with joy. Her expression changed as Logan got out of the car.

"Come in," she instructed, scowling at Logan.

Dee led them to a study, where the walls were covered with maps and awards in frames. Seated on a burgundy leather sofa, Logan asked Lara to explain. She summarised her father's letters and handed them across to Dee.

"It's a good story," said Dee, glancing down at the letters. "And I can see it working as a documentary, but I'm not making any new television series at the moment."

"Did you work on *Logan's Jungle Trek*?" asked Rufus, with a gleam in his eyes.

"Yes, my father's company produced it," Dee responded.

"So, you can tell us what he did to get his show cancelled?"

As Dee opened her mouth to speak, Logan hastily interjected.

"Ha, we don't have time to go into that now, Joe," he said, shooting a meaningful look at Rufus. "Anyway, Dee, we're not looking for a TV show, we need a flight in your plane to Egypt to find Dr Abdul Faruk to help us find the treasure."

Dee looked at Logan as if a second head had just grown out of his neck. She threw her head back and laughed heartily, her thick curls bouncing on her back. After a moment, she noticed that the faces in front of her were solemn.

"Oh," she said. "You were *actually* being serious?"

"Come on, Dee," persisted Logan. "We always said we'd go on a big adventure one day ... well, this is it," he said with his arms outstretched.

"What about these kids? What does their mother think of all this?"

"My mother's away," said Lara vaguely, "so Logan's been staying at our house."

"So ... all three of you would be coming as well?"

"And Barney," Lara added.

"No way ... it's crazy enough taking three kids to Egypt with no notice, but a dog as well?"

Barney got up from the floor and walked to the desk chair where Dee was seated. He licked her ankles, making her giggle, then jumped heavily into her lap, almost causing her to fall onto the floor.

"You're *adorable*," cried Dee as she hugged Barney. "I'll probably regret this ... and it's not going to be easy ... but I'm going to get you all into Cairo."

Rufus whooped for joy as Logan fist-pumped the air. Lara and Tom grinned at each other, thrilled.

"I need to make arrangements … meet me at Biggin Hill airport tomorrow morning. Come early … four a.m."

"Dee … I swear to you, you'll not regret this," promised Logan.

"Oh, get out of here before I change my mind!"

Chapter 7
Destination: Cairo

Later that afternoon, as they returned home and got out of the car, Logan noticed movement from across the street.

"Lots of nosy people around here," he observed, as two faces appeared behind a twitching curtain opposite the house, then ducked.

"That's just Daisy and her sister," said Lara, shaking her head.

Logan spent most of the evening upstairs getting his phone account reconnected, whilst Lara, Tom and Rufus discussed the trip ahead. Barney was making the most of Mrs Jacobs' absence and messily chomped on a humungous bone on his favourite rug in the living room.

"Have you got a passport?" Lara asked Tom, who had never left the UK before.

"Yeah, there's a school day trip to France next term," he replied, "I've got my passport with me. I can't believe my first time abroad is going to be with you guys, in Egypt." Even saying the word 'Egypt' gave him visions of pyramids, tombs and camels wandering across the sand. Even if meeting Abdul came to a dead-end, he could not wait to experience the sights and sounds of a new country.

The phone rang in the hall and Rufus ran to answer it.

"It was Auntie Sarah," he said, returning back into the room a few minutes later. "She asked if we had anything nice planned and I said we're going to meet one of Logan's friends from TV and we might be out of the house a lot, so she might not get through if she calls."

"That's *technically* true," said Tom.

"But it's not the full story," said Lara, fidgeting with her hands. "She'd never let us go and meet Abdul in person, she'd probably email him, not get a response, then we'd never find out *anything*. What are you going to tell your mum, Tom?"

"She mainly texts me asking if I've had a good day and what I've had to eat," he said, feeling a little guilty. "I can still text her back while we're in Egypt."

Everyone went to bed early ahead of their trip to the airport in the middle of the night.

At three a.m., Lara, Rufus and Tom eagerly jumped out of their beds and woke up Logan, who was still groggy. Within minutes, they had grabbed their packed bags and cases and were in the Jeep on the way to the airport.

It felt exciting to be starting their journey in pitch black darkness. But disaster soon struck. About halfway to the airport, Logan's Jeep spluttered to a halt.

"I can't believe this piece of junk has conked out *now*," cried Rufus. "Awful timing."

"Maybe I can fix it?" said Logan, who proceeded to spend five minutes trying to find the switch to open the car bonnet and succeeded only in opening the car boot and accidentally beeping the horn four times.

"I can try," said Tom quietly.

"Well, you can't be much worse than Mr Bean here," quipped Rufus. Logan's cheeks flushed pink and he stepped aside from the driver's seat.

Tom pressed a switch that released the bonnet with a click. Using his phone as a torch, he nimbly tinkered about with the engine.

"Try turning the key," he called out.

Logan turned the key and the engine roared back to life. Lara and Rufus gave a cheer.

"How did you do that?" asked Rufus.

"I learnt from my dad," Tom said while climbing back into the Jeep.

A few miles further up the road they arrived at Biggin Hill airport.

A sleepy-looking security guard wandered up to the car.

"Charter flight?" he asked with a yawn.

"We're meeting Dee Okoye," said Logan.

"Go through," he waved his hand then stopped. "Wait, do you have papers for that dog?"

"Yes?" said Logan with a blank expression.

"Can I see them?"

"They're online," said Rufus quickly. "We submitted them through the portal."

"Oh … okay," said the security guard. He walked back to his cubicle and pressed a switch to open the gate.

"Good thing you knew about that online portal, Joe," said Logan.

"I made it up … now step on it before he realises!"

Logan put his foot down and sped towards the carpark. Dee was waiting for them by the building entrance.

"Come inside and get through security," she said. "I've got clearance for Barney." Everyone followed Dee inside the airport building and speedily got through security checks. They proceeded out the back into a buggy driven by a member of airport staff towards Dee's plane. They each climbed up the stairs to enter the plane, which was decked out with four leather seats facing each other with tables in-between and a large sofa. Rufus opened his mouth in amazement.

"This is *so* cool!" he gasped, flinging himself into a seat. "Tom, take a photo of me on your phone so I can show everyone at school."

As Tom took photos of Rufus posing, Barney jumped on the sofa and Dee handed Logan everyone's passports that she had grouped together. Logan opened them and handed Tom and Lara theirs. He frowned at Rufus' passport.

"Joe … your name's wrong on your passport," he said. "It says Rufus Kexley, not Joe King."

Lara, Tom and Rufus burst out laughing.

"His name isn't really Joe," said Lara.

"What?" said Logan, still confused. "But I've been calling him Joe for two days!"

"Oh my goodness," said Dee as she swotted Logan's arm lightly with her passport. "Don't tell me you fell for that one … Joe King … *joking* …"

"Oh my …" Logan blused. "Not funny, kids."

Rufus, Lara and Tom laughed all the more, and eventually, a smile crept onto Logan's face.

"Let's get going now," said Dee, climbing into the cockpit. "This is Clive," she said, indicating the co-pilot in his late fifties sitting next to her.

The stairs were cleared away from the side of the aircraft and Dee steered the plane towards the runway. The engines rumbled loudly as the plane's speed increased and it took off into the night sky.

"We're off," said Lara, smiling and rubbing Barney's fur as a feeling of anticipation swept across her. "Next stop: Cairo!"

Chapter 8
Cairo

An hour into their journey, Logan fell asleep on the sofa at the back of the plane. Lara, Rufus, Tom and Barney watched the sun rising in the sky, bathing the sea beneath them in orange and pink light. They found a fridge full of drinks, snacks and sandwiches, which they feasted on as they talked about the trip ahead.

After several hours, Dee prepared the plane for landing.

"Look out the window on the left," she called out, as she banked the aircraft above the River Nile.

Lara, Rufus and Tom gazed out at the Great Pyramid of Giza and the surrounding pyramids below.

"It still looks massive," gasped Rufus, "even from up here."

About twenty minutes later, Dee and Clive masterfully landed the plane and everyone except Clive got out to head towards the security checks. Clive stayed behind to refill the plane's fuel before finding a hotel close to the airport.

Inside the airport security area, an official pulled the group to one side.

"I will take your dog and put him in a cage," he said, pointing at Barney. "He needs checks."

Lara pulled Barney towards her so he was sitting close to her feet.

Dee got out a large brown envelope from her rucksack.

"Here," she said, passing it to the official. "We've got papers and … something extra to help out," she said with a wink.

The security guard took the papers out of the envelope and threw them over his shoulder where they landed in the bin. He pulled out a wad of green US dollars and stuffed them into his pocket.

"I will complete the checks from here," he said, walking around Lara and peering at Barney, who was growling softly. "Okay, checks complete."

With sighs of relief, they moved on from the security area where they were crowded by hordes of taxi drivers and luggage carriers vying for work. Confidently leading the way, Dee ignored the loud drivers trying to get her attention and strode towards a much quieter man at the back of the crowd, who had given up competing with the others.

"Can you fit us all in your taxi?" she asked.

"Yes," he said, his eyes lighting up in surprise. "I drive a large taxi."

"Great, we'll need you for the next day or two at least," she said. "Lead the way, please."

Not believing his luck, the taxi driver shuffled quickly towards his heavily dented people carrier parked outside the airport building. He slid open the door and the six got in.

"What's your name?" Dee asked the driver.

"Seth, ma'am," he said. Everyone introduced themselves.

"Pleased to meet you all," said Seth, who had already forgotten everyone's names. "Where would you like to go first?"

"The Egyptian Museum," said Dee. "As quick as you can."

Chapter 9
The Egyptian Museum

Lara, Rufus and Tom had never experienced traffic like the roads in Cairo. The white lines separating the three lanes were completely ignored as five rows of cars weaved their way dangerously in and out.

Tom, whose only experience of traffic was when a slow tractor caused a build-up of cars, or a herd of sheep escaped into the country lanes, could not take his eyes off the mayhem.

"It's carnage," said Rufus, poking his head dangerously out of the window, alongside Barney. "Look over there! That car's about to get hit."

"So are you," cried Lara, yanking her cousin back into the car. "Barney, get your head back in here too!"

A red car in front of them was pulling out of its lane as a faster car crashed into it from behind. There was a series of car honks and a lot of shouting before both drivers sped on. Seth, well used to driving in Cairo, deftly weaved the car back and forth on the way to the museum. Logan felt slightly queasy and closed his eyes, hoping that they would arrive soon.

After about an hour, Seth parked the car close to the museum. They walked around the corner to a statue of a sphinx, with its human head and cat-like body guarding the entrance to the museum. The museum was a gigantic building painted in a clay-like orange colour.

"I'll wait here out of the sun with Barney," said Lara, who was itching to enter the museum but did not want to cause trouble by bringing a dog inside.

"But it's your dad's legacy," said Tom. "And you know more about Egyptology than the rest of us put together."

"I can look after the dog," offered Seth. "I know a café around the corner where I can fetch some water for him."

"I'll stay with you," said Dee. "Logan, your phone's working now, right? Text me when you're finished. I've got your Egyptian pounds for the entrance fees."

Dee handed Logan some Egyptian notes and headed off with Seth and Barney.

Logan, Lara, Rufus and Tom headed inside the museum. They paid for their entrance and asked for Dr Abdul Faruk's office.

"It's in the basement," said the man selling admissions. "But no tourists are allowed there."

"Can you tell him we're here, please?" asked Lara. "Tell him we're the family of Lucas Jacobs."

"Okay, I'll tell him. Stay on the ground floor please."

The four walked through to a grand hall housing many statues and artefacts. At the end of the hallway and up a flight of stairs were impressive statues of a pharaoh and queen, seated on thrones overlooking the floor. They walked through the large room, reading some of the descriptions.

"There's *so* much here," exclaimed Rufus. "We could have some immense games of hide and seek."

"Mum said once that if you spent ten seconds looking at every item on display, it would take two weeks," said Lara.

"And there's even more in the basement," said a voice behind them. They turned to see a man in his forties with tanned skin and dark hair, dressed in a white shirt and dark trousers. "I'm Abdul," he said quietly, with a furtive glance around him. "Come quickly, this way."

Abdul hurried across the side of the hallway and opened a door, ushering everyone through. He led them down a staircase into a basement. Lara was amazed at the ancient Egyptian items crammed in around her but did not have time to study them in detail as they had to almost run to keep up with Abdul. He turned into a narrower corridor and opened the door to an office, closing the door behind them.

"You should not be here," he warned, after taking a seat at the desk. "There are people who have been following me for years, spying on my calls and emails. They've even bugged my office."

"Hadn't we better talk somewhere else then?" asked Tom, looking behind him half-expecting enemies to come crashing through the door.

"This is my colleague's office, not mine," explained Abdul. "And anyway, you are wasting your time. I cannot tell you anything worth knowing."

"That's not true," protested Lara, with a fiery flash in her eyes. "You wrote to my dad, Lucas Jacobs. It's right here."

Lara handed the letters across to Abdul, who flicked through them.

"I thought he had destroyed these," he said, shaking his head. "This is dangerous knowledge to have."

"But it was important to my brother," said Logan. "And he's not here anymore, so we need to pick up where he left off."

Abdul sighed.

"I cannot help you with this," he said, shrugging his shoulders. "The danger is too great, and I have a family to think of. Please, I *urge* you, give this up and go home."

Everyone sat in silence for a moment, feeling defeated and disappointed.

"What was my dad like?" Lara asked, her voice barely above a whisper. "I was too young when he died to remember him."

"Lucas?" asked Abdul, a faint smile appearing on his face at the memory. "He was a dear friend. I never knew anyone so brave but also kind. And so smart, he always worked things out. I miss him very much."

"What do you think he would be saying if he were in the room with us now?" said Lara.

"Probably the same thing you're saying now," said Abdul after a pause. "He loved the thrill of a new discovery, despite the dangers."

"Just tell us *something*," pleaded Rufus. "If you were going to look for the treasure in a temple, where would you start?"

"I already know the temple in which the treasure is located," said Abdul. "The Temple of Akhmim."

Chapter 10
Making Plans

Rufus jumped out of his seat.

"Great!" he cried. "We'll go to the Temple of Akhmim."

"It's not that easy," said Lara, staring at the floor. "The Temple of Akhmim is buried underground. It has a whole city built on top of it. Nobody can get inside."

"It's true," added Abdul. "Lucas believed that there was another entrance into the temple, but I don't think he ever found it."

"We can't give up now," said Rufus.

"Where would you start looking … if you wanted to?" Lara asked.

Abdul sighed as he scanned the papers in front of him for a few moments.

"Some of the hieroglyphs here are from Dayr al-Bahri, I think. If you must continue with this … which I *do not* advise, then start there."

Everyone thanked Abdul and felt relieved that their journey had not come to an end.

"I must ask one thing …" said Abdul, getting up from his chair to open the door. "When I let you back out into the main hallway, don't head straight for the exit. It will look too conspicuous. Go amongst the crowds of tourists for a while, it may help if you are being watched. Do not speak of any of this in public. Do not trust anyone."

The group glanced at each other before nodding at Abdul.

He led the way back through the basement and up the stairs in a hurry, almost shoving the four back out onto the museum's ground floor and slamming the door shut behind them.

"What do we do now?" asked Logan.

"Let's go to the second floor, to the Tutankhamun exhibit," suggested Lara. "There will be loads of tourists there. Why don't you text Dee and tell her we'll be out in half an hour?"

Logan, Lara, Rufus and Tom climbed the stairs up to the second floor, where a large group of tourists were stood in front of Egypt's most recognisable treasure – the Mask of Tutankhamun.

"It's solid gold," exclaimed Rufus, staring with fascination.

"I can't believe it's over three thousand years old," said Tom, reading the description. "It looks so ... perfect."

They spent an enjoyable half an hour scanning the exhibit, marvelling at the treasures discovered in Tutankhamun's tomb in 1922. Many of the items felt very personal, such as jewellery and stools with carvings, which gave Lara a shivery feeling inside as she imagined the items being used by the boy king.

As they headed towards the exit, Logan turned to Lara, Rufus and Tom.

"Guys, let's not mention the stuff about danger and spies to Dee," he said. "She's different to me ... she's ... what's the word?"

"Intelligent?" suggested Lara.

"Successful?" added Tom.

"Better looking?" quipped Rufus.

"No ... well yeah, all of those are probably true," said Logan, blushing. "But she's kind of cautious, you know? She's ..."

"Responsible?" said Lara.

"*That's* the word I'm looking for. She wouldn't let you kids come along if she thought it was dangerous.

Not that I want to put you guys in danger, err … I just want to finish what my brother started."

The sun beamed down on them as they exited the museum through the gift shop. Seth, Dee and Barney were standing under the shade of a tree waiting for them. Barney was overjoyed to be reunited with Lara and jumped up, hugging her waist excitedly. Dee had a slightly concerned expression.

"As you were walking down here, there were two guys behind you, *really* close," she said. "Even Barney growled a bit to start with. It looked weird … I thought they were coming down here with you, but they saw us then headed off over there."

They turned to see two men wearing dark suits and hats hurrying off to the side. One turned and met their gaze, then quickened his pace.

"Strange," said Logan. "Let's get back to the car, we've got news. Seth, can we go somewhere for lunch?"

"I know just the place."

Seth drove everyone a short distance away and parked the taxi on a road by the River Nile.

"I don't see any restaurants around here," complained Rufus, whose stomach had been rumbling loudly in the car.

"They're all on the boats," said Seth. "This one is my favourite; it's run by friends of mine."

Seth bypassed several large ships packed full of tourists enjoying their lunch and took the group to a much smaller, run-down boat. They walked up the gangway into a restaurant that was completely empty apart from one snoring man with his head rested on a table.

"Eman!" shouted Seth, shaking the man's shoulders. "Wake up! I've brought you customers."

Eman woke up with a start. "Welcome, everyone," he said, frantically getting up from his chair and wiping a long trail of drool from his chin. Dee turned her head away in disgust. "Please, please, take a seat over here. I will give you the best table in the whole restaurant, by the window."

"*That's* good of him," quipped Rufus to Tom and Lara, staring at all the empty seats.

"You have a dog?" Eman questioned, tucking his shirt into his trousers to cover up his rotund belly.

"Yes …" said Lara, staring at the large man. "You're *looking* at him."

"Okay … it is okay … so long as no other customers make a complaint." Eman walked to the kitchen, tripping over a chair on the way there.

"Are there loads of invisible customers we can't see?" asked Rufus, peering underneath the table cloths.

After everyone had sat down and Barney had settled under Lara's feet, Eman came out with a jug of water and a handful of menus. He handed out the menus and filled up a glass of water for each person. Spotting a fly buzzing above the table, he snatched Logan's menu from him and flung it about, missing the fly but knocking Logan's glass of water all over him. Dee snorted behind her menu.

"It's okay," said Logan amiably. "The sun will soon dry it off."

"This is a very good restaurant," said Seth, looking at his menu.

"Yeah, it shows," said Rufus, rolling his eyes.

"Thank you, young sir," said Eman eagerly. "What will you all have to eat?"

"I'm not really sure of the choices," said Dee, frowning at the menu. "Seth, what would you recommend?"

"Koshary is my favourite," Seth replied. "It's traditional, Egyptian food: rice, macaroni, lentils, chickpeas, onions. There's also Shawarma: chicken or beef with spices in a wrap."

"Let's get a bunch of stuff and try some of each," said Logan. Everyone agreed and Eman scuttled back to the kitchen with their order.

"Does Eman cook the food?" asked Tom.

"No," said Seth, "his wife does all the cooking."

"Thank crumbs for that," said Rufus.

"As if it would stop *you*," said Lara, who knew her cousin's enormous appetite that always seemed at odds with his small build.

"I would like to go and say hello to Eman's wife, please excuse me." Seth got up to go into the kitchen. While he was gone, Lara quickly filled Dee in on the conversation with Abdul at the museum, leaving out all of his warnings.

"Where is Dayr al-Bahri?" asked Dee. "Is it close to Cairo?"

"No," said Lara, "it's in Luxor."

"We can't go by my plane. I spoke to Clive while you were all in the museum, there's a small fault and it's going to take two days to get the right part to sort it out. Let me see what other options there are."

Dee opened up her phone and started browsing.

"Bus … no, too long. Flights … fully booked. Train … night train. There's an overnight train we can get on, it leaves at five past midnight and should get us into Luxor around nine a.m. We can board at the station in Giza."

An overnight train sounded very exciting to Lara, Rufus and Tom.

Eman, his wife and Seth emerged from the kitchen carrying plates of food. The smells were very appetising. Lara, Tom and Dee tried not to look at the food stains all over Eman's shirt, while Logan and Rufus, who were too hungry to notice, dug in.

"This is delicious," said Rufus, piling more food onto his plate. Lara separated some chicken and fed it to Barney under the table, who gently scooped it from her hands.

Lunch was followed by a selection of desserts. There were sweet pastries stuffed with nuts and covered in syrup; rice pudding; sweet dough balls drizzled with honey and a selection of Egyptian cakes.

Everyone enjoyed the food, particularly Logan and Rufus, who devoured twice as much as everyone else. Lara, giving her stomach a chance to digest everything, paused and glanced out of the window. Her gaze rested on something disturbing.

"Those two men from the museum are by your car," she exclaimed to Seth.

Everyone stared out of the window to spot the backs of the two men – identifiable by their suits and hats – snapping a picture of the number plate. One man turned around and looked up at the boat. His face was tanned and mostly covered by a beard. He saw the group staring back at him and nudged his companion. They both hurried off around the corner.

"I don't like it," said Dee, frowning. "It looks like they followed us down here for some reason."

"A few people follow tourists to ask for money," said Seth, shaking his head. "It is a great shame and bad for tourism."

"They didn't look like they needed money," said Lara, "judging by their clothes."

"There are money-making scams in Cairo," said Seth. "I'll check the car before we head off, just as a precaution," he added, noticing the nervous look on Dee's face.

Chapter 11
The Bazaar

After lunch, there were still several hours to spare until the night train to Luxor. Dee did not want to purchase tickets right away in case they were being followed, so she asked Seth to take them somewhere to buy supplies for their journey. Seth took them to Khan el-Khalili, a shopping district bustling with locals and tourists.

They walked past many stalls selling brightly coloured and intricately patterned rugs, as well as stalls selling hundreds of souvenir pyramids and miniature pharaohs.

"I've got food for Barney, but I need somewhere I can get more bottled water and a bone," said Lara. Logan, Seth and Dee were talking to a trader about Egyptian spices.

"Don't go too far off," said Dee, "we'll go over to that coffee shop in a minute and wait for you there."

Lara, Tom, Rufus and Barney headed down the street. At each shop they passed, shop owners eagerly fired friendly questions at them and offered cups of tea.

"We've got to keep moving or we'll never find the shop we want," said Tom. They moved at a faster pace, quickly scanning the contents of each shop they went by. Lara looked behind her and shrieked.

"We're being followed!" she gasped. Tom and Rufus turned around to see the two men from outside the boat, alongside three others, rapidly making their way down the street behind them. The four broke into a run, dashing between the crowds. As Tom looked back over his shoulder, the five men had also broken into a sprint and were gaining ground.

"We've got to lose them!" cried Tom. "Turn left."

They fled down a small alley then took another turn, almost bumping into two men carrying boxes of goods into a shop. The five men turned the corner and barged straight into the pair, sending boxes of spices flying into the air, forming a great cloud of orange dust. They did not stop to apologise and continued the chase.

Tom, Rufus, Lara and Barney continued turning left and right, until they came to a dead-end. The sound of footsteps and shouting got louder behind them.

"This way!" yelled Rufus, charging into a souvenir shop. They ran inside and pelted through the shop into the private quarters at the back, much to the shock of the owner at the till. They found themselves in a kitchen with a backdoor. Thankfully it was unlocked, allowing them to exit into the small yard and out the back gate.

They breathlessly continued on, their hearts pounding in their chests, hoping to lose the five men. Turning left at the end of the back street into another alley, they stopped.

"Another dead-end," said Lara as they faced a high wall with apartment buildings on each side. "Can we go back?" The footsteps got louder, and Barney growled, preparing to defend his friends.

"This way!" yelled a voice from above. "Up *here*."

They looked up to see a girl leaning out of a door at the top of metal stairs. The four ran up the stairs, almost tripping over themselves as they dived through the doorway. The girl followed them and closed the door behind her, milliseconds before the five men appeared around the corner.

They lay on the ground, exhausted and wheezing for breath, except for Barney who launched himself at their rescuer in gratitude.

The girl giggled and petted him, her large brown eyes sparkling with joy. She got up to take a peek out of the window.

"They've gone," she said with a sigh of relief.

Lara, Tom and Rufus looked around them. They were in a small room furnished simply with a rug, an old couch and a chair covered in blankets. They turned their gaze to the girl standing in a blue T-shirt and jeans, who had long dark hair, like Lara's. She was smaller than Lara and Tom, around the same height as Rufus, although she looked a little younger.

"Thank you," said Tom. "You really helped us out there."

"It's okay," replied the girl. "Do you want something to drink? I'll get something for your dog too, he looks thirsty." She went into the kitchen and filled a bowl with water for Barney. She poured four glasses of Coca Cola and put them on a tray.

"Here you go." She placed the drinks on a small side table and sat next to it, on the floor.

Lara, Tom and Rufus thanked her and took their drinks.

"Are you here on holiday?" asked the girl, tilting her head to the side.

"Sort of," said Rufus.

"What are your names?"

"I'm Rufus, this is my cousin, Lara. Our mate, Tom, and Barney. What's your name?"

"Maye."

"Funny," said Lara, "Karim's little sister is called Maye too."

Maye's mouth opened wide.

"My brother is called Karim," she gasped. "He's in England, is that where you're from?"

"Yes," said Lara in surprise. "Maybe it's a coincidence though …"

"He works at a university," said Maye.

"Did you send him camomile tea recently?" asked Tom.

"*Yes*," screamed Maye, hugging her knees tight into her chest. "Are you those people who found the treasure? In the summer?"

"That's us," said Rufus, smiling broadly. He never tired of people bringing up their adventures over the summer or their appearance on the evening news.

They talked excitedly about Karim, Kexley Castle and the current escapade that they had found themselves in.

"Wow," said Maye in awe, "my brother said the news in England called you guys 'The Adventurers', and now you're in the middle of *another* adventure."

"We'd better be heading back to find my uncle and Dee," said Lara, looking up at a clock on the wall. "We've been gone a while and I still need to buy bottled water for our train ride and a bone for Barney."

"I'll show you where to get those," said Maye. "Then if those men find you again, I can help you lose them. Let's go."

Chapter 12
The Sound and Light Show

Maye led her new friends to a small supermarket where they bought drinks and snacks. The owner was delighted to have visitors and wanted them to all stay and take tea with him, but they politely refused. When they made it back to the coffee shop, Dee was seated at a table with Logan and Seth and jumped up quickly when she saw the group come in.

"*Where* have you been? You've been gone ages," she scolded. "Logan, aren't you going to say something?"

Logan was relaxing in a chair, emptying his fourth cup of coffee.

"I told you they'd be back," he said, shrugging his shoulders.

Dee grunted in exasperation and sat back down.

"Sorry, it took us a while to get what we needed," said Rufus, whilst pulling out a chair to sit down on.

"And who's this one?" Dee looked at Maye.

"This is Maye, Karim's little sister," said Lara. "We ran into her in the market."

"I can come with you to Luxor," said Maye, nodding quickly.

"Oh no, we've got enough minors on this trip already," Dee shook her head. She looked at Logan for back-up. "Logan, will you say something? We can't keep accumulating kids!"

"Eh?" Logan had been staring longingly at the pastry display by the counter. Dee shot him a furious look.

"I'm sorry, but you can't come with us and your family will be expecting you home."

Maye folded her arms sullenly, but did not argue with Dee.

"What are we doing before the train?" asked Tom, hoping to break the tension around the table.

"Well," said Seth, "I suggested taking you all to the Sound and Light Show at Giza. There's enough time to see it before your train. That way you can see the pyramids during your stay in Cairo."

Tom, Rufus and Lara were thrilled with the suggestion and the group soon left the café. Seth dropped Maye back at her family's apartment. She very unwillingly got out and returned up the metal stairs.

"Thank you for all your help, Maye," called Lara out of the window. "We won't forget you."

"No, you won't," Maye yelled back with a smile as she closed the door of the apartment.

Darkness fell suddenly as they arrived at the Giza plateau. As the show started, an old-fashioned voice boomed out of the speakers, telling the story of the last remaining ancient wonder of the world. Multi-coloured lights illuminated the gigantic pyramids and the giant sphinx. Lara had seen pictures of these wonders many times in her mother's university books, but sitting in front of them in the cool Cairo air, with Barney nuzzling against her and Rufus and Tom seated either side of her, was a magical experience.

As the show was coming to an end, Lara, Rufus and Tom felt a shadow flit past them. Barney whimpered and looked behind them.

"Do you think we're being followed still?" whispered Tom as his eyes scanned the audience around them.

"Barney would be growling if those men were anywhere around," said Lara.

After the show, Seth took the group back to his taxi and drove to Giza Station. They walked through the entrance with its decorative columns, and Seth went with Dee to buy tickets.

"I keep feeling a shadow going past me," said Rufus, spinning to check behind his back for the fifth time.

Seth and Dee returned.

"The train should be arriving in the next five minutes, then leaving in half an hour," said Seth, patting Barney's head. "Good luck in the rest of your travels, my friends."

Everyone thanked Seth warmly and Dee handed him a generous tip, which he looked embarrassed about and tried to give back, despite the amount being more than he would usually make in a week.

"Why's he not taking it?" whispered Rufus to Lara and Tom in amazement. "He could get some of those dents in his car patched up."

"Pride, I guess," observed Tom. "Seth's a nice guy."

Dee and Logan eventually managed to persuade Seth to take the money. He thanked them, blushing profusely before returning to his cab.

They made their way to the correct platform just as a long green and cream-coloured train arrived. An official disembarked to check their tickets.

"No dogs allowed," he said, pointing at Barney.

"He's not ours," said Rufus, flapping his hands at Barney. "Beat it. Scram. Vamoose!"

"Your rooms are in the fourth carriage along."

Barney whimpered and padded away, his tail low between his legs. Lara opened her mouth to object and Rufus shoved her into the train.

"What are you *do*—" started Lara.

"Shhh," cautioned Tom. "He's moving the other way now."

The ticket collector moved to a carriage further forward to check more tickets. Lara, realising her cousin's plan, softly whistled. Barney, who had been hiding behind a bin, bounded towards the train and leapt through the door, knocking over the whole group like dominoes.

"Oof!" cried Logan, who was at the bottom of the pile.

They walked to their carriage and found their four rooms. Logan's room was towards the front. Tom and Rufus were sharing a room in the middle, Lara and Barney's room was next door and Dee's room came last at the back. All of the rooms were the same, with two seats, a small window and a tiny sink. A steward came along and pulled out the two bunk beds in each room.

Lara and Barney, too excited to sleep, stayed in Rufus and Tom's room, where they all crowded on the bottom bunk and talked about the day's events.

Dee knocked on the door.

"Goodnight you lot," she said. "Logan's getting to bed already. Lara, don't stay too long in here before you get to bed, it's been a long day."

They wished Dee goodnight and a few minutes later the train began to ease out of Giza Station.

"We're on our way!" Rufus cried as they looked out of the small window into the night sky.

Chapter 13
Visitors in the Night

About an hour into their journey, a storm struck, sending streaks of light across the desert terrain outside the window. For the four, it made the night train even more exciting. A steward knocked on the door and brought hot meals with rice, breaded chicken, and vegetables. Unlike the ticket collector, he was overjoyed to see Barney and brought extra food for the hungry dog. Rufus and Barney scoffed most of the dinner whilst Tom and Lara ate sandwiches they had bought at the market.

"I don't know how you do it," said Lara, staring at her cousin, who was demolishing food at a faster rate than Barney.

"Are you eating those cakes?" Rufus asked, his mouth full of chicken.

After the meal, Rufus needed to find the bathroom. Thirty seconds after leaving the room he knocked on the door again.

"I can't go in the toilet in our carriage," he whispered, holding his nose. "It *stinks*. Logan must have been in there."

"Well he eats at the same speed as you, so that doesn't surprise me," snapped Lara.

A rumble of thunder roared outside the train.

"Is that thunder or your stomach?" joked Tom.

"Why'd you come back here?" said Lara. "There'll be another one in the next carriage."

"I think there's someone in there, I saw a shadow."

"Go into the smelly bathroom then and hold your breath," said Lara, losing patience. "I don't know what you expect us to do about it."

"I *can't*," Rufus protested. "It's rancid! I'd pass out on the floor. It smells like a million rotten eggs blended with skunk farts, sprinkled with horse's—"

"*Alright,* I've heard enough." Lara's face contorted with disgust. "And it's starting to waft over here with the door open. Take Barney with you, he'll let you know if there are other people around."

Barney, keen to explore and stretch his legs, eagerly padded along by Rufus' side. They hurried past the stinky bathroom into the next carriage.

Outside the next bathroom, Rufus noticed an engaged sign on the lock, so he carried on through the carriage and opened another door that led into an empty dining room. The lights were off, but he could see through the frequent flashes of lightning that the room was decorated in old-world style, with green leather seats and mahogany tables. At the other end of the dining carriage was a door into a corridor with a bathroom sign outside.

After using the facilities, Rufus re-entered the dining car with Barney. He noticed a torch light illuminating the bar he was standing next to. Grabbing Barney's collar, they both ducked behind a seat just as a group of three men entered the dining car from the direction of the bedroom carriages.

The men murmured to each other in a language that Rufus could not understand. He kept hold of Barney and listened hard. Suddenly, he recognised two words from the conversation and froze. One of the men had just mentioned 'Lucas' and 'Abdul'. The small boy wished he had a way to translate what the men were saying.

A downpour of rain started to hammer the windows as the lightning eased for a few moments. Peering around the seat, Rufus recognised the man facing towards him from the chase in the marketplace. As he stared in shock, there was a movement behind the men as the handle of the door from which they had entered began to move. A sudden flash of lightning revealed the person opening the door.

Maye! thought Rufus, as the girl's eyes widened in fear of the men who looked like they did not want to be disturbed. *What is she doing here?*

Hearing the door handle, the men spun around and marched towards the door. Thinking on his feet, Rufus opened the opposite door and slammed it hard, flinging himself back behind the seat where he and Barney were concealed in the darkness.

Jumping round in surprise, the men flashed their torches towards the door next to Rufus and Barney and rushed through it into the next carriage. Maye came into the dining car and almost shrieked in surprise as Barney launched himself on her in delight.

"Rufus! Barney!"

"Quick, we've got to go before they come back!"

Rufus, Maye and Barney fled through the dining car as they heard shouts from the corridor behind them. They tore through the next two carriages and Rufus pounded the door to his and Tom's bedroom. Tom opened the door and stared in shock as Rufus charged into the room followed by Barney and Maye.

"Keep quiet," Rufus whispered as he closed the door behind him.

The five stood in anticipation as they heard the door to their carriage swing open and voices through the corridor. The footsteps and voices became more distant as the men moved on through the train.

Rufus heaved a sigh of relief.

"What's going on?" asked Lara. "Maye, what on earth are you doing here?"

Chapter 14
Maye

"I took the bus down to the Sound and Light Show," Maye explained, seating herself on the bottom bunk as Barney cosied up next to her. "I didn't let you see me in case that woman sent me home again."

"Dee, you mean," added Lara.

"Yeah, her. Anyway, after you got to Giza Station, I didn't have enough money to get a ticket; I spent all my money getting a taxi to follow you there. So, I jumped on the train just as it was about to leave. I kept having to hide whenever the conductor came by, so I've mostly been in the bathroom next to the dining car."

"It was engaged when me and Barney walked past," said Rufus, impressed with Maye's level of scheming.

"What about your mum and dad?" asked Tom, looking unsure. "Won't they be worried?"

"I told them I'm going to my auntie's apartment," Maye replied.

"That's not right, Maye," said Tom with a blush.

Rufus, shrugged his shoulders. "We can hardly talk. Lara's mum and your mum and dad think we're back in Swindlebrook. As for my mum … she stopped caring a long time ago."

Lara had a flashback to the five minutes Auntie Rachel had spent with her son during the summer after a long absence abroad and winced. She knew her aunt was still living in Los Angeles and that she had not phoned or sent any letters or emails in the past few months.

"You'll have to sleep in my room next door," said Lara, "there's not much else we can do now. It's getting pretty late."

"Do you think we should tell Logan and Dee that those guys are on the train?" asked Tom.

Lara and Rufus considered for a few moments.

"They might say we have to go home if we tell them," said Rufus. "We'll just have to make sure we lose them somehow."

Lara felt a pang of doubt in her stomach. She knew her mum would be angry at the danger that they were putting themselves in, but she couldn't bear the thought of abandoning the search that her father had started so many years ago.

It was past one o'clock in the morning and after checking that the coast was clear, Lara, Barney and Maye crept into the cabin next door. It was a rough ride to Luxor over the next few hours and the five frequently woke up with a jump as the train sped over a bump in the tracks. Maye almost fell out of the top bunk as the train jolted sharply. Finally, the sun began to rise in the sky and Tom and Rufus joined Lara, Maye and Barney as they ate their breakfast of croissants.

Dee knocked on the door and Tom let her in.

"We've got about an hour left until –" Dee stopped mid-sentence and frowned at the additional passenger. "What are *you* doing here?"

"Maye came onboard last night," said Tom quickly, before Maye had the chance to say anything rude.

Logan entered the room behind Dee.

"Anyone got any croissants left over?" he asked, stretching his arms and yawning.

Everyone paused for a moment and stared at Logan.

"What?" he asked.

"Have you not noticed anything?" snapped Dee. "*Anyone?*"

"No," said Logan, staring around the room and up at the ceiling. "What am I looking at?"

"Not at the ceiling, you clown! The kid from the market is back here again."

"Oh, hi Maye." Logan grinned broadly. Maye waved sheepishly. "So, nobody answered me about croissants?"

Dee left the room with a huff, flapping her hands above her head as she went.

Chapter 15
Dayr al-Bahri

The train stopped at Luxor Station, where busy crowds lined the platforms. Rufus, Lara, Tom, Maye and Barney fled from the train as soon as the doors opened, hoping to make a quick exit before they could be followed again. Dee and Logan followed behind, hurrying to keep up with the five ahead.

Outside the station, Tom was in front of the others and found a minibus taxi.

"Dayr al-Bahri please," he said to the taxi driver once everyone had jumped in.

Rufus looked over his shoulder and saw the men from the dining carriage running out of the station.

"Make it snappy!" he yelled. The driver pulled out of the taxi bay and zoomed up the street, leaving a cloud of dust behind them that made the men cough and splutter.

"What's with the rush, guys?" asked Dee. "I thought we could head to a hotel first and put our bags away."

"Good thinking," said Logan. "Excuse me, is there a hotel nearby that will allow dogs?" he asked the taxi driver.

The taxi driver drove to a quiet hotel with walls patterned in different colours of paint.

After checking in, the group were led through the lobby into a square with a swimming pool in the middle. The porter showed them to their four rooms.

Maye stood by the door of the room that she would be sharing with Lara and Barney, her mouth open in amazement.

"I've never stayed in a hotel before," she said, as her eyes took in everything around her. "This is *so* cool!" She hopped from the bathroom to the window, marvelling at everything she saw.

Lara felt a twang of self-consciousness as her initial first impression was that the twin-bedded room, whilst spotlessly clean, was slightly old-fashioned. She had stayed in hotels many times, either on holiday or sometimes when her mum had needed to travel somewhere to give a lecture. She watched Maye's excitement and wondered when it was that she had started to take things like travelling and hotel rooms for granted. Barney was just as excited as Maye and eagerly sniffed every corner of the room, determined to find every smell.

Next door, Rufus and Tom were just as enthusiastic as Maye.

"I've never stayed in a hotel before," said Tom, turning on the large, dated tube TV and flicking through the channels.

"I can't wait to pull some pranks around here," said Rufus, staring out at the pool as entertaining schemes formed in his head.

Dee and Logan grouped everyone together to catch a taxi to Dayr al-Bahri.

"Best we go while it's still early morning," said Dee. "Before too many tourists turn up."

A short ride later, after paying a small admissions fee, they were gathered outside a huge three-story temple built on the side of a cliff, rectangular in shape with two flights of steps in the centre of the structure. Each floor held numerous openings and eight statues guarded the top floor.

"It's the Temple of Hatshepsut," explained Lara, who did not need a guidebook to navigate her way around the site. "Queen Hatshepsut had it built to tell the story of her life and reign."

They walked up the stairs and explored the temple. Many of the paintings on the walls appeared intact.

Lara held up the pictures from her fathers' papers and compared them to the paintings on the wall.

"This is one," she said eventually, after they had travelled the entire floor space of the vast temple.

They gathered around a picture of an Egyptian holding two blue shapes out to another figure with the head of a falcon.

Rufus squinted at the hieroglyph. "Why's that guy's head shaped like a bird?"

"That's Horus," said Lara, pointing. "He was a god, a protector."

"I thought you said this temple was for a queen," said Tom. "But all these pictures are of men."

"That's because after Hatshepsut died, a male pharaoh called Thutmosis took over her temple. He got rid of all the statues of her and replaced the paintings. He almost completely wiped out her memory."

"What a pig," spat Dee, disgusted.

"Swine," added Maye. She and Dee looked at each other in surprise at having agreed on something for the first time.

"Why would he be with this Horus guy?" asked Rufus.

"Because he wanted protection, I guess," said Lara. "Plus, the eye of Horus was said to be powerful, there's an eye on that drawing with a line into Thutmosis. Maybe that's meant to mean something."

"But it doesn't tell us much about the missing treasure, does it?" asked Rufus, frantically scanning the drawing for some sort of clue.

"No … the only connection I can think of is that the treasure was displaced from the royal tombs, just like Hatshepsut was displaced from this temple," said Lara, who was also studying the painting hard.

They walked around for a while longer but could not see any hint of a clue.

"There's probably nothing here anyway, it's too touristy for stuff to be hidden," said Logan. The temple had started to fill up with visitors as they walked around. "What about the place where the mummies were found? Is that close to here?"

"It's right around the corner of this cliff. I looked it up on Tom's phone," said Lara. "I don't think we can get into it though, it's not open to tourists."

"That's never stopped us before!" Rufus rubbed his palms together.

Everyone looked at Dee, expecting her to object.

"Well…" Dee considered. "We've come this far, and there's *nothing* else for us to go on… so let's go."

Barney led the way as they scurried around the cliff over the sand and rocks.

"It's a massive area to cover," said Logan. "Let's split up in pairs and have a look round. Dee, let's start from over there."

Maye and Rufus took one direction whilst Tom and Lara took another. Half an hour passed as they carefully searched.

"Barney," called Lara, pouring some water into a dish from her backpack. "Have a drink."

Barney lapped up the water thirstily as Lara and Tom took a seat on a rock and drank from their flasks.

"This is crazy, isn't it," said Lara. "Even if we find it, we won't be able to get in."

Before Tom could answer, Barney began barking loudly and scratching the ground.

"He must have seen a beetle or something," said Tom.

"Be *careful*, Barney," yelled Lara, starting to panic that there might be a poisonous bug or snake in the sand. She and Tom jumped up to grab him, but he sped past them. They turned their backs as he appeared to vanish in the ground.

"Barney!" screamed Lara, running after him towards a deep cavern.

Chapter 16
The Royal Cache

Tom grabbed Lara just as she was about to launch herself into the space below. They both landed backwards with a thud.

"Don't be an idiot, Lara!" yelled Tom. "See how deep it is down there?"

"But Barney fell down there!" wailed Lara, trying to release her arm from Tom's grip.

"He *jumped*. And you know he's a hundred times more sure-footed than any of us, he probably scrambled his way down."

Lara peered over the edge of the hole, which was too dark to see the bottom.

"Barney? Barney!" they both called.

Seconds later Barney woofed back in response. Lara wiped tears of relief from her face.

"Barney, are you hurt?" she whimpered.

There was no response.

"I can hear his footsteps," said Tom. "If he's walking around, he's probably okay."

"How on earth are we going to get him out?"

"What's going on here?" said Logan, who had rushed back to join his niece and Tom after hearing screaming. Dee, Maye and Rufus were close behind. "You found the Royal Cache?"

"Barney jumped down there," gasped Lara, "we need to get him out. Now!"

"We'll have to go back to the temple and get help," said Dee.

"Wait." Logan threw his rucksack on the floor and opened it to pull out a long rope and climbing equipment.

"You brought something *useful?*" Dee stared wide-eyed at Logan.

"Well, you don't have to look so shocked about it," said Logan, feeling offended. "I was on *Logan's Jungle Trek* for two years, you know. I like to think I picked up *some* skills."

Dee kept quiet as she tried and failed to think of something nice to say about Logan's time on *Jungle Trek*.

Lara hastily tried to attach a climbing belt to her waist. "I'm going down there first!"

"No, you're not," said Logan, taking the belt from her. "Your mum would kill me if anything happened."

"But Barney's down there!" she yelled, pointing to the hole.

"Just let him go first." Tom gently took Lara's arm. "Barney will be alright, Lara. We'll get him out."

Logan fixed the rope to an anchor and threw the other end into the cave. He was about to climb down it as Dee interrupted him.

"Wait!" She tugged the rope slightly and the anchor slid along the ground. "You should *always* test a rope before putting your body weight onto it."

"I knew that." Logan's eyes darted to the floor. "I was just testing *you.*"

Dee and Logan sorted out the anchor and tested the rope again. It was sturdy.

"Shine this torch down as I go," he instructed, passing one of his torches to Dee.

Logan travelled down the entrance to the Royal Cache, bouncing his feet against a few ridges in the rock. When he reached the bottom, Barney jumped up and hugged his waist, grateful to see a friend in the dark cave.

"Well?" yelled Lara down the hole. "How's Barney?"

"He's absolutely fine," Logan hollered, his voice echoing around the cave. "The dirt on the ground here is soft, it must have cushioned his landing. We'll just explore down here, and you can pull us up later."

This was an unpopular suggestion with everyone at the cave entrance.

"No way!"

"Get out of town!"

"Are you *kidding* me?"

"Logan!"

"Alright, alright," said Logan. He unhooked himself and everyone travelled down the rock, starting with Lara and ending with Dee. Lara squeezed Barney into a hug as he showered her with licks.

They shone their torches to see two chambers on either side of them. Rufus, always anxious to be first, pushed his way past Logan and led the way into the chamber on the left.

"It's completely empty," said Rufus. Let's try the other way."

They trooped back in the other direction which led to a small opening, less than half the size of the chamber.

"Well, if there's anything to find, it'll be in the bigger room," said Logan. He turned around, followed by Dee. Rufus was about to join them when he noticed Lara staring transfixed at a spot in the wall in front of her, with a puzzled expression.

"What is it?" he asked, following Lara's gaze in case he had missed anything.

"I've just got a weird feeling in this area that I didn't have in the chamber," she said with a slight shiver. "I can't explain it ... it almost feels like I've been here before."

Rufus, Tom and Maye started to feel around the walls and the floor. Lara stayed in the same spot, still holding a look of intense concentration.

"Aren't you going to help?" said Rufus, who was quickly growing impatient. "Nothing's going to jump out from that wall with you staring at it."

Something Rufus said triggered a thought in Lara's mind. She stepped forward and placed her hand on a deep crack in the wall. Tracing the line with her fingers, she saw that it led all the way up to the ceiling.

"Tom, lift me up," she said. "I think there's a gap up there."

Tom crouched down and lifted Lara onto his shoulders. The tips of her fingers touched the point where the crack got wider.

"I need more reach," she said.

Maye pelted to the other chamber and returned, dragging Logan by the arm.

"Lift Lara up," she ordered.

"Bossy, this kid," exclaimed Logan to himself.

Lara let herself down and climbed onto Logan's shoulders. This time she could reach her hand into the crevice. Her fingers touched dirt and she squealed as an insect of some kind crawled over her wrist. Determined to continue, she carried on feeling and searching. When she had pushed her hand as far into the gap as it would go, she felt something.

"I can feel paper!" she cried.

"Get it out, get it *out*," yelled Rufus, jumping up and down in excitement.

"It's hard … my hand won't go far enough in."

"Let me try," said Rufus, yanking Lara's legs from Logan's chest.

With even more resolve, Lara gritted her teeth and stretched her fingers as far as she could into the tight gap. Using her middle fingernail, she scraped the dusty paper one millimetre at a time until finally, she was able to clasp the corner with two fingers.

"I've got it!"

Chapter 17
The Letter

Lara pulled a thick envelope from the wall and waved it over her head in triumph.

Logan let her down and she stared down at the once-white envelope that was caked in grit and dust.

"Maye, can you go and get Dee, please?" asked Logan.

"I don't want to," Maye replied, her eyes fixed on the envelope.

"Why won't any of you kids listen to me?" asked Logan. Nobody responded except Barney, who woofed. "Barney, get Dee." Logan pointed towards the corridor. "Dee. Other room."

Barney sat down and woofed again.

"Dee... Go find!" Logan swept both hands towards his right. "Go ... find. *Find.*"

Barney stared at Logan and tilted his head to one side, which made Rufus and Maye chuckle.

"He's wondering what you're talking about," said Maye, giggling.

"Great," Logan flapped his arms in exasperation, "even the dog doesn't listen to me."

"Barney, go fetch Dee," said Lara. She smiled as Barney stood up and trotted down the corridor.

A few moments later, Dee followed Barney into the opening.

"He wouldn't stop barking at me until I followed— hey, what's that?" asked Dee, noticing the envelope.

Lara opened it and stared at her father's handwriting, which she read aloud.

"Logan,

If you're reading this then I'm no longer around and you've looked through those papers I gave you. I'm onto something, I know it. I believe there is a secret entrance to the Temple of Akhmim and all my research points to treasure from the royal tombs being hidden there.

There is another group trying to get there first. They're dangerous and will stop at nothing to discover the valuables and sell them on the black market. Even just a few of the artefacts expected to be hidden there could be worth millions.

There is one person who left the group and went into hiding – called Ali. I believe Ali knows something about the secret entrance. I have never met Ali, all I know is that there is a connection to boats and carpentry. The last I heard, Ali lives in a small fishing village north of Girga. I am sorry I cannot share more information with you, but Ali's whereabouts have remained hidden for almost ten years.

All that remains for me to say, my brother, is if you are reading this – and I hope you never have to - give my family all my love. My darling wife Sarah and little Lara are worth more to me than all the riches of Egypt.

Your brother,

Lucas"

Lara's voice faltered as she read the last few lines. She swallowed hard.

"Well," she said, after clearing her throat. "It doesn't give us much to go on."

"It doesn't give us *anything*," complained Rufus with a stomp of his foot. "There could be a million guys called Ali in Egypt."

"And we don't even know where he is," said Dee. "I hate to say this, but I think we should call it a day."

"Well, I didn't say that," Rufus backtracked quickly. "Yeah, there's a million Ali's, but how many of them work with boats?"

"I have to do this," said Logan, his eyes steadily fixed on Dee. "It's what Lucas wanted … he always looked out for me growing up and I never did anything for him in return. I understand if you don't want to join me, maybe you can take the kids home and I'll carry on from here."

Lara stepped forward. "Forget it, Uncle Logan. I'm connected too in this, there's no way you're going without me."

"Or me," said Tom, stepping forward to stand next to Lara.

"Or me," added Rufus, joining her other side.

"Or me," said Maye, who did not have space to stand next to the others and sat on the floor next to Barney in solidarity.

"*You?*" snapped Dee. "Honestly, I don't even know how you're still here?"

Maye shot a look so fuming that even Dee started to feel uncomfortable and looked away.

"Fine," she conceived, turning towards the tunnel entrance. "We'll all go to look for Ali. *One day* and that's it. I'm not spending weeks out here interviewing fishermen. And we've got to get these kids back home soon, anyway."

Tom, Lara and Rufus nudged each other in excitement.

"Should we hire a car?" asked Logan.

"Not a car," said Dee, with a smile. "We're getting a boat."

Chapter 18
Back at the Hotel

Everyone climbed up the rope into the warm October sun. Logan went last, carrying Barney over one shoulder as the others pulled the rope up. They returned to the entrance of the Temple of Hatshepsut and caught a cab back to the hotel.

Inside their rooms, they were in for a shock.

"Someone's been through our stuff," cried Rufus, his eyes darting around the room. "I had two bags of Haribo sweets next to my bed, now they're gone."

"I think my jacket has been moved as well," said Tom. "It could be the cleaner moving stuff though?"

"They wouldn't clean our rooms right after we've just checked in."

They quickly packed their things back into their suitcases and checked to see if anything was missing.

"All my stuff's still here," said Tom. "I'm glad I had my passport in my backpack."

"Thank you, thank you, *thank you*," said Rufus, lifting his hands up to the ceiling. "They put my Haribo back in my suitcase."

"Hey, someone's been in our rooms," said Lara, entering the boys' room with Maye. "My toothpaste has moved. They went through your stuff too?"

"Someone's been in our rooms?" asked Logan, standing with Dee in the doorway.

"I don't like this," said Dee. "Lucas' letter said that there was a dangerous group of people... what if it's those men who were sniffing about outside the Egyptian Museum and the restaurant?"

"We should get on the boat today," suggested Tom. "If we're on the river we'll be constantly moving and they won't be able to trace us as easily."

"You're right," said Dee. "For all we know, they could be watching now."

"Wait ..." Rufus looked straight past Dee. "Don't turn around ... there are two guys on the other side of the pool ... I think they're watching us."

Logan was about to turn around when Maye kicked him swiftly in the shin.

"Owww!" he groaned.

"Sorry! You were going to turn around."

"Next time, just tell me," he said, rubbing his leg.

"We need a distraction …" said Rufus, his hand on his chin. "Logan, Dee, in five minutes we'll go to the pool and cause a scene. You two watch us on the deck chairs, then when they're distracted, go to reception, check us out of the hotel and get a cab ready. If we push our suitcases out the windows to the front of the hotel, they won't notice us moving them and we can grab them on the way out."

Five minutes later, everyone met at the pool area in their swimming costumes, as if they hadn't noticed anything amiss in their rooms. One of the men in the deck chairs opposite briefly peered over his newspaper, then hid behind it again.

Four German children were playing a game of water basketball.

"Hey," bellowed Rufus. "Can we play?"

One of the boys threw the ball to Rufus. He dive-bombed into the pool with it, sending splashes of water over towards the two strangers. Tom, Lara, Maye and Barney took their cue from Rufus and jumped in all at once, this time showering the two men and their newspapers in water.

"Hey!" shouted one of them. "Be careful."

"Let's play," yelled Rufus. He pretended to aim the ball at the basket and sent it straight towards the two men, hitting the smaller man's head with a donk. Before he had the chance to protest, Barney leapt out of the pool and went to grab the ball, shaking his wet coat all over the place.

"Stop this!" shouted the man hit by the ball, his clothes saturated.

"Let's play tag," Maye lightly tapped the tallest German boy. "You're it."

Maye jumped out of the pool and was chased round and round the deck chairs by the boy and Barney. Everyone else got out of the pool and joined in the game. The men continued protesting. One started flapping his newspaper at the German boy (who was now busy chasing his sister) and the other mopped his lap with a towel after Maye had knocked his drink into it.

Tom and Lara stopped for breath behind the changing room shed.

"Look," said Lara, pointing at the empty deck chairs where Logan and Dee had sat. "They've gone already, we need to get out of here."

Tom peered behind the shed to see Rufus furtively unscrewing the umbrella behind the two men. He caught Rufus' eye and pointed to the hotel lobby. Rufus let go of the umbrella, which slid down onto the two men below, causing even more mayhem and angry voices. He caught Maye's attention as she ran past shrieking with laughter, and along with Barney, they pelted to the hotel entrance.

Tom and Lara were slightly ahead of them and saw Dee and Logan getting into a large taxi. Within seconds, everyone had dived into the car and it sped off into the distance.

Chapter 19
Aboard The Miranda

The Port of Luxor was packed full of boats of all shapes and sizes. There were sailing boats, long wooden boats, rowing boats, speedboats and a few expensive-looking yachts.

Dee had phoned Clive who was still with her plane at Cairo Airport. He had been able to arrange for the hire of a speedboat through a contact he knew. She had also persuaded Maye, after much protesting, to write down the number to her parents' apartment in Cairo, so that they could be told where their daughter really was.

"I can arrange for the man I'm collecting the boat from to put Maye back on the train to Cairo," offered Dee to Maye's father. "We likely won't be back there for another couple of days."

"Oh, there's no need for that. Maye's mother and I have enjoyed the break, Maye can be a little trying sometimes. Keep her with you until you return, that's fine with us."

"Well …" Dee stumbled, thinking of a polite way to tell Maye's parents that she had found their daughter pretty 'trying' as well. She looked down at Maye who was sitting slumped on the deck, staring into the water, her feet hanging over the edge. She looked so pitiful that Barney strolled up and gave her an enormous lick on the face and placed his front paws in her lap. Dee sighed. "Okay, that's fine, when we get back to Cairo, I'll make sure a driver can take her home."

Clive's Egyptian contact was looking out for the group and as he saw them walking along the deck, he jumped down from his boat to meet them.

"Welcome to *The Miranda*," he said, pointing to the painted name on the boat. "She's all ship shape and ready to go. There are two bedrooms, a kitchen and bathroom downstairs… but rather a lot of you?"

"We can sleep on the deck or inside the lounge area," suggested Tom. "Are there sleeping bags? And a mosquito net?"

"There's a mosquito net, I'll grab more supplies from the office. Give me a few minutes and make yourselves comfortable onboard."

Everyone climbed onboard and started to explore. Rufus headed straight for the captain's room and grabbed the captain's hat that was placed next to the steering wheel.

"*Yes*," he cried, fist pumping the air. He found a microphone and speaker and turned them on.

"This is your captain speaking," he announced in a deep voice. "Welcome aboard *The Miranda*. Rule number one: no stinking out the cabin bathroom ... yes, I'm talking to *you*, Logan. Rule number two: I will be addressed as Captain Rufus at all times. Rule number three—"

"Give me that!" Logan yanked the captain's hat from Rufus' head and smiling nervously at the small crowd of onlookers who was staring up at them from the deck below.

"Anyone who farts onboard must immediately walk the plank..."

"Turn that *off*," hissed Logan, pulling Rufus out of the captain's room.

"Is that man coming with us?" Lara asked Dee.

"No, one of us will need to drive the boat."

"I can," said Logan, who had joined them back on the deck with Rufus.

"Oh no," Dee shook her head. "Anyone but you, Logan. Remember you crashed that speedboat on the Amazon river on *Logan's Jungle Trek*? That was the start of the *incident*."

"Will someone *please* tell us what happened on *Logan's Jungle Trek*," pleaded Rufus. "It's not fair that you two know and we don't. Share the wealth."

Dee threw her head back and laughed. "It was so … *funny* …" tears started to form in her eyes. "Everything was going wrong for Logan! Starting with the—"

"Okay, okay," interrupted Logan, his cheeks flushing pink. "So, who's driving the boat if not me then?"

"*Meee*," cried Rufus, resolving to return to the subject of *Logan's Jungle Trek* when Logan wasn't around.

"Not you," said Lara, scrunching her face in disapproval. "Your crash record is just as bad as Logan's. Remember that time at go-karting—"

"I can do it," offered Tom quickly, trying to prevent an argument between his two friends.

"Have you driven a boat before?" asked Logan.

"Well, yeah, I used to help out the fishermen back in Cornwall sometimes."

"That's settled then," said Dee. "Tom's the captain. Lara, you're pretty sensible, maybe you can go with him and read the maps?"

Tom smiled very slightly as Rufus folded his arms and huffed in exasperation.

The boat's owner came back with another man carrying extra supplies of blankets and pillows. He took Tom and Lara into the captain's office and showed them all of the controls and how they worked.

"Where are you headed first?" he asked.

"South, towards Aswan," Lara replied.

"Well, the boat has enough fuel to get you there and back, and you'll find extra supplies in the bunker over there. Safe travels."

The man hopped off the side of the boat and untied it from the mooring, throwing the ropes across to Lara.

Tom started up the engine and slowly guided the boat out of the port heading south.

"You know we shouldn't really be going south, right?" asked Lara, once they were out of earshot from the people standing on the deck.

"I know," Tom replied. "I took your hint… if those people following us come up here, we want the boat hire guys to say they saw us heading south. When we get past this busy part of the river, I'll turn *The Miranda* around and we can head back north."

A few minutes later, when the river had quietened, Tom swung the boat around and accelerated back north.

"Did you go the wrong way?" Rufus joined Tom and Lara. "And has anyone seen where Logan put my captain's hat?"

"He's wearing it." Tom pointed behind them where Logan was sitting with the cap on over aviator sunglasses, talking to Dee and Maye.

"Good thing Daisy's not here," said Lara. "She'd be going all gooey over him!"

At that moment, a much bigger ship passed close to them in the other direction, sending a gust of wind over the deck that knocked Logan's hat from his head. Barney swiftly jumped up and grabbed it in his mouth.

"Over here Barney," called Rufus. Barney ran over and gave him the hat.

"Hey!" shouted Logan, "give that back."

"It's mine now!" Rufus planted the cap firmly on his head.

Logan shrugged and carried on looking out over the water.

"So how come you went the wrong way?" Rufus asked Tom.

"We didn't ... it was a decoy in case anyone was watching or if anyone gets asked where we went."

"But won't they see us now going in the other direction?"

"They won't be looking for our boat," said Lara, "and they'll be dealing with other tourists, so they might not notice."

"So which way are we going now?" Rufus peered at Lara's map.

"North," she answered, "back in the direction of Cairo, but we don't need to go that far."

"If this is north, how come the water is flowing in the direction we're going?"

"Not all rivers flow south," Tom explained. "They can go north or south, as long as it's downhill."

"The Nile starts up in the mountains in Africa," said Maye, joining the others. "It flows downhill north through Egypt. Karim told me that."

"So, when do we start looking for Ali?" asked Rufus.

"When we get past Girga," said Lara. "The letter said he was in a village north of Girga."

Chapter 20
The Nile

Tom steered the boat along the Nile, passing through both populated towns as well as quieter areas with farmland on one side of the river. They occasionally passed other ships and boats coming towards them in the opposite direction. Rufus took great delight in waving at the tourist cruise ships until the passengers on board waved back, then contorting his face and sticking his tongue out until they all looked away nervously. Occasionally, they came across fishing boats, occupied by very tanned men of all ages, who chatted loudly amongst themselves and called out greetings to the group aboard *The Miranda*.

"Do you think we should be asking some of these fishermen if they know Ali?" asked Tom.

"We're not close enough to Girga yet," said Lara, "and this lot are too noisy for any of them to be someone hiding his identity from a gang."

As they reached Girga, the waters became busier again and more buildings appeared next to the river. The sun was starting to set in the west and the sky was filled with pink and orange light that reflected across the water.

"It's going to get dark soon," said Rufus, "I think we should stop somewhere and eat. We won't find Ali in the dark, most of the fishermen will have gone home already."

Once outside of the busy city, Tom stopped the boat and released the anchor down next to a small island. He released the boat's metal gangway onto the land. Rufus and Lara found a picnic rug and spread it onto the ground. They searched the food cupboards in the kitchen and found fresh bread, different spreads and a variety of snacks and cakes.

After they'd laid everything out on the picnic rug, Tom was about to fetch Dee and Logan when Lara put out a hand to stop him.

"Wait," she said. "The two of them have been sitting out at the front of the boat all afternoon."

"So what?" said Rufus. "There's nowhere else they can go, it's not like they're going to take a dip in the river."

"Can't you *see*?" Lara sighed. "This is the first time they've got on with each other this whole trip without Logan doing something stupid and Dee telling him off for it! Look at them – I've never seen Dee laugh and smile so much. I don't think we should disturb them."

"Well they're going to have to eat," said Tom. "Why don't we take some of this food over there then leave them to it?"

Tom and Lara took some of the food over with some plates and cutlery. Maye found another picnic rug in the kitchen while Rufus located a bottle of wine and two glasses.

"What's all this?" questioned Dee as they silently placed the picnic next to her. "Are we all eating out here?"

"You two are," said Lara. "We're eating on the little beach over there. See you later." She nudged Maye, Tom and Rufus away before Dee and Logan had the chance to say anything else.

"What are they doing?" asked Lara, when they were sitting back down on the sand. "I can't see them from here."

"They're still smiling and laughing," Tom reported, craning his neck to see. "Logan's opening the wine ... well, he's struggling to open the wine ... he's just fired the cork into his forehead ... Dee's checking he's alright ... now they're both laughing again."

"*Boring,*" Rufus complained, with an exaggerated yawn. "Can't we talk about something else? If I wanted to watch a load of bad dates I'd go and visit my mum in L.A."

"How are we going to find Ali tomorrow?" asked Maye, who had also lost interest in Logan and Dee.

"I really don't know." A frown line appeared on Lara's forehead. "It's been eleven years since my dad wrote that letter, Ali could have moved on since then. Because the letter said he's in a fishing village, I'm hoping he's one of the fishermen out on the river. We might have to get talking to the fishermen tomorrow."

By the time dinner had been packed away the sky was pitch black. The late October air had turned cool.

"Who's having the two bedrooms?" asked Dee.

"You and Logan can have them," said Lara. "There's enough room out in the living area for the five of us with our sleeping bags."

After a day of exploring the Luxor desert and boating down the Nile, everyone was feeling tired. Lara picked one of the couches to place her sleeping bag on. Barney kept trying and failing to squeeze into the sleeping bag alongside her. Soon everyone was fast asleep, dreaming a jumbled mixture of hidden tombs, overnight trains and being followed down the Nile by unseen enemies.

Chapter 21
Looking for Ali

Barney was the first to wake up the next morning with a soft growl. There was something happening outside of the boat, he could hear it. He jumped down from the sofa where he had been sleeping at Lara's feet and pounced on top of Rufus so that he could look out of the window onto the river.

"Oof," moaned Rufus, "What are you doing, Barney?"

The collie started barking and raced to the door, pounding it with his paws.

By this time, everyone had woken up and Tom, who was closest to the door, opened it slightly. His eyes caught something alarming behind the door and he slammed it back shut before Barney could charge onto the deck.

"What is it?" asked Logan, emerging from his bedroom.

"You'd better see for yourself," uttered Tom, staring through the glass in fascination.

"Aaaaaaaaahhhhhhh," screamed Logan, jumping back from the glass and springing onto the couch. "Crocodile!"

"A Nile crocodile," said Tom, his brown eyes gleaming in awe. "It must be at least fifteen feet long!"

"*Awesome*," yelled Rufus, joining Tom's side along with Lara and Maye. They stared at the prehistoric-looking creature that was slowly easing himself across the deck towards the door.

"We left the gangway down on the sand last night," said Lara, clapping her hand against her forehead.

"Do *something*," urged Logan, still standing on the sofa armed with a cushion.

"You're the survival expert," said Dee, who had joined the group. "You can't leave it to the kids!"

"Woof," barked Barney, still scratching at the door.

"Or the dog."

"Err …" said Logan, dropping the cushion and wringing his hands. "Err …"

"We need some food to lure it back onto the ground," Lara suggested calmly.

"What she said," added Logan.

Rufus ran to the fridge and started flinging the contents onto the floor.

"Cakes ... butter ... milk ... steaks – that'll do the trick." He tore open a pack of four raw ribeye steaks. "Let me up through the skylight, I need to get out that way."

"Oh no," said Dee. "I'm not having a kid swallowed by a croc. Logan, you go."

"So, it's okay if *I* get swallowed by a croc?" The scornful look on Dee's face answered his question. "Okay, okay."

Logan nervously snatched the pack of steaks from Rufus' hand and hauled himself up through the skylight. He shuffled slowly towards the edge of the roof, stumbled and slipped to the ground.

"Don't drop the steaks," ordered Lara from the window.

Getting up and breathing heavily, Logan quickly flung a steak out of the packet with a shaky hand. It landed into the river with a plop.

"That was awful," yelled Rufus.

"Do better," spat Maye.

"Stop *yelling* at me," replied Logan. Taking a deep breath, he flung another steak. It landed straight into the mouth of the crocodile, who received it with a quick snap of his jaws.

Before Logan had to face the pressure of throwing the third steak, he felt a firm hand grasp his shaking forearm.

"I'll have a go," said Tom gently. He took the two steaks and flung one of them onto the bottom of the gangway with ease.

"He's not moving," whispered Logan, clutching Tom's shoulder.

After a few tense moments, the crocodile turned and heaved his large body down the gangway. Once he had neared the bottom and gulped down the steak, Tom launched the last steak onto the sand, as far away as he could. To everyone's relief, the crocodile continued hulking his mass onto the sand away from the boat.

Logan and Tom jumped down from the roof and lifted the gangway up from the ground. Dee, Rufus and Maye hoisted up the anchor whilst Lara started up the boat's engine.

"That was *so* cool," said Rufus, using Tom's phone to snap a few pictures of the crocodile as they sped away.

"We're past Girga now," said Lara, once they had left the crocodile far behind. "So, once we come across more people we should stop and talk to them."

The river became less congested with boats the further they got away from the town of Girga, with farmland opening up again on the side of the riverbank.

They saw a couple of fishermen in sailing boats and stopped to talk to them.

"Excuse me," said Logan. "Do you know where we can find Ali?"

"Which Ali?" said one of the men.

Nobody really had an answer to this.

"How many do you know?" asked Tom after a pause.

The man hesitated for a few moments, using his fingers to count.

"Fourteen," he answered. Everyone groaned.

"Wait," said Lara, pulling her father's letter out of her pocket and scanning the contents. "Do any of them work with boats and carpentry? With wood?"

"No," said the man flatly. "Would you like to buy fish?"

They thanked him and politely declined the fish.

Two hours later, after stopping to ask six more fishermen, everyone in the boat was feeling downhearted.

"I don't think I can take much more of this," Dee flopped into one of the deck seats. "It has to be one of the most popular names in this part of the world, yet none of them seems to fit the tiny description we have."

Maye pointed to a man standing by the riverside with a small boy who looked around five years old and an older girl. "Let's ask those people."

"Well, it can't hurt," said Tom, steering the boat towards the bank.

"Hello there," Logan called.

"Hello," said the girl, who looked around twelve.

"Hi," added the man.

"It's a beautiful day on the river," said Logan.

"Yes, it is," replied the man with a friendly smile. "Are you on holiday with your family? Do you need help with any directions?"

"Err, yes we're visiting from the UK," said Logan. "There is something you might be able to help us with. My brother used to live in Egypt, over ten years ago now. He knew someone called Ali who lived in these parts and was good with carpentry. Does that ring any bells?"

Lara, Tom and Rufus felt sure that a spark of awareness lit up in the man's eyes, but he shook his head firmly.

"No, I'm afraid it does not."

"Are you sure?" Logan persisted. "My brother was certain there was a chap called Ali who made boats."

"Boats! Boats!" cried the young boy, suddenly clutching his hands in excitement. "Ali boats! Ali boats!"

"No, we don't know an Ali who makes boats," said the man, quickly scooping the child up in his arms and turning his back to walk away. The girl looked a little doubtful.

"Do you know?" asked Lara.

"No, she doesn't," snapped the man. "Come on, Rashida."

A woman came towards the man and children with long dark hair speckled with grey. She was dressed rather like the man on the riverbank, in a white shirt and linen trousers.

"Ali! Ali boats!" screamed the young boy, pointing at the woman. "Ali!"

Chapter 22
Ali

"Ali is a *woman*?" Tom questioned out loud. "Lara, can that be right?"

"It must be," Lara stared down at the letter and rapidly scanned the contents. "Look ... Dad never once said 'he' or 'him' ... he must have had a hunch."

The man spoke to the woman in Arabic and tried to pull her away from the river. Maye called out to them and they started a heated conversation back and forth in Arabic. The others on the boat waited impatiently, wishing they could understand the dialogue taking place between the Egyptians.

"What do you think Maye's saying?" Lara whispered to Tom.

"I don't know ... but it seems to be working," said Tom. The woman climbed onto the boat and walked towards them.

"You are Lucas' daughter?" she said, her brown eyes staring straight at Lara, who nodded. "I know he was looking for me … many years ago. I will explain everything. Let's go inside."

The man and his two children waited outside whilst everyone else crowded into the living area.

Logan offered a cup of tea, which was declined.

"My name is Aaliyah," said the woman, sitting on one of the couches. She sighed heavily. "My father was a boat-maker and taught me how to make sailing boats and rowing boats. I started building boats with him when I was twelve. He got into trouble with money and borrowed some from bad people. He wanted to repay them with boats, but they wanted more, and he had to leave home often to work for them. My father became ill and I had to run his errands instead, passing things back and forth between different locations. My father had always told them my name was Ali, thinking it would help protect my identity from the gang. Whenever I went on these jobs, I would cover my hair in a turban, so that if people saw me at a distance, they would think I was a boy. I was always collecting documents and packages from different hiding places; I didn't have to meet people. One day, my father passed away while I was out on a job. After his funeral, I packed my things and left our home. They have not been able to find me since."

Everyone stared in amazement at Aaliyah, her story sounded like one from a film. She pulled her hair away from her face, looking tired.

"Why would they still be looking for you?" asked Dee quietly. "Did you owe them more money?"

"No," Aaliyah replied. "It wasn't that. I know too much … and I kept information from them that they badly wanted. That they *still* want."

"What is it?" gasped Rufus, on the edge of his seat. "What do you know?"

"I know how to find the secret entrance to the Temple of Akhmim."

Chapter 23
The Map

"Tell us!" Rufus clutched his hands together. "How can we find the secret entrance?"

Aaliyah hesitated and looked towards the door.

"Wait a minute," said Lara, who was afraid that Rufus' pushiness would make Aaliyah leave. "How did you find out?"

"I found a map amongst my father's belongings that I took with me. I don't know where he got it from or how long he'd had it, or if he even drew it himself."

"Why didn't you hand it over to the authorities?" asked Dee.

"It is very hard knowing who to trust. Even within the authorities, maps and artefacts can end up in the wrong hands. My father must have known what the map was and what it meant, yet he kept it hidden all those years even when he had money trouble with the gang. That's why I will never let them have it."

"But you didn't destroy it?" gasped Rufus, horrified at the thought.

"No, I hoped one day an opportunity would come along to reopen the temple with the right people. People I can trust." Aaliyah gave a slight smile.

"You can trust us," said Logan. "We're not going to steal the contents of the temple … although some extra cash would be nice …" Dee glared at Logan. "No, no, I mean we wouldn't take anything, we just want to continue the search my brother started."

"Can I really trust you?" Aaliyah leaned forward in her chair and stared deep into Logan's eyes. "There could be danger, the gang have members spying throughout Akhmim. And you have four children with you."

"They're the perfect cover," said Logan. "Nobody would think we're searching for the secret entrance with four kids and a dog in tow."

"I need to speak to my husband … and get the map. Wait half an hour. If I return, I will come with you. If not, you must go home and forget this conversation."

Aaliyah got up abruptly and left the boat, starting a heated discussion with her husband as they walked towards their house.

"He doesn't want her to go," said Maye, peering over the side of the boat.

"Well, we'll have to wait and see I guess," said Dee, who was half hoping for and half dreading Aaliyah's return.

Everyone waited anxiously on board the boat, unable to focus on anything other than the story that Aaliyah had told them. Even Rufus was too distracted to eat his usual third helping of breakfast. Lara took Barney for a short walk along the riverfront, and by the time she came back, there was still no sign of Aaliyah.

"It's been half an hour now," said Dee. "I think we should go."

"Hold on," said Rufus, squinting his eyes. "There's someone coming … it's Aaliyah!"

Everyone turned and saw a figure in the far distance. Aaliyah was returning with a rucksack. Her hair was covered in a turban.

"We'll attract less attention if onlookers think I'm a male tour guide," she explained, boarding the boat.

"Did you bring the map?" asked Rufus.

"Yes." Aaliyah took an envelope out from her rucksack and handed it to him. "You can take a look if you want … just be careful."

The adults went inside the cabin while everyone else headed to the captain's area. Tom started up the boat towards Akhmim, while Rufus, Lara and Maye poured over the map. The River Nile was shown at one end of the city as well as a few buildings with names in Arabic. One of them was circled and had a dotted line leading to a drawing of two statues.

"The statues must be at the entrance of the temple," said Lara. "They were discovered in the early eighties but nobody has been able to get inside. Maye, what's this building that looks connected to the statues?"

"It's a hospital." Maye furrowed her eyebrows. "But that doesn't make sense … lots of people must use that building every day, so how can it be hiding a secret entrance that nobody's found yet?"

"We'll find it," said Rufus with a confident grin. "Hey Tom, can't you drive this boat faster?"

"I'm going pretty fast already," Tom replied. He felt just as eager to arrive and start the search. "We'll be there in an hour or so."

Chapter 24
A Surprise

Tom found a place to stop the boat in the city of Akhmim. Everyone was excited to start exploring, although Aaliyah had been on her phone for the past ten minutes, having another angry conversation with her husband.

"Come *on*," Rufus whined. "We're ready to go."

Dee shook her head at him.

"I'll be a few minutes," Aaliyah said, rolling her eyes in apology. "Why don't you wait for me in that coffee shop and I'll come over when I'm done."

Everyone left the boat and went into the café, where they bought drinks and pastries. Rufus, Tom, Maye and Lara slurped fruit smoothies while Barney attracted the attention of the young waitress, who showered him with attention and brought him some dog biscuits and a bowl of water. Logan and Dee talked amongst themselves and frequently glanced back at the boat.

"I don't like it," said Dee, once she had finished her coffee. "Do you think she's going to back out?"

"It's been about twenty minutes now hasn't it?" Logan checked his watch. "I'll go back and see what's going on."

"Don't *you* go," snapped Dee. "You're bound to say the wrong thing."

"I have *excellent* negotiation skills Dee," insisted Logan. "Remember that time on *Logan's Jungle Trek* when we met those annoyed aborigines Down Under and I calmed the situation down?"

"You did not. You just confused everyone by talking in a fake Australian accent and making weird hand gestures."

"Well it worked, didn't it?"

"I hardly think it's going to in this situation."

"Why are you so down on me all the time?" Logan crossed his arms and slumped in his chair in a manner that reminded Lara very much of Rufus.

Maye stood up and placed her hands on her hips. "Why are you two arguing like big kids? Nobody cares about *Logan's Jungle Pecs.*"

"Trek," shrieked Lara, wincing at the thought of a show dedicated to Logan's physique. "For pity's sake, don't give him ideas."

"Hey, I think it could work," said Logan, flexing and admiring his muscles.

"I think I'm going to be sick," groaned Dee with a grimace.

"Get out of here and check the boat!" Maye banged her fist on the table. Logan and Dee were so shocked at the small girl's ferocity that they both got up and went to the door.

"Watch my bag on the chair," said Dee, looking over her shoulder on their way out. "We'll be back in five. Don't go wandering off."

"Well, so much for romance blossoming between those two," observed Tom as the door shut behind them. "Back to hating each other after five minutes."

"Oh, I prefer it," said Rufus, slurping the last of his smoothie.

Minutes later, the five began to feel bored. Rufus stared up at the ceiling while Maye put her head on the table. Tom and Lara finished their smoothies and Barney, feeling full from the treats, lay down by their feet.

"They're taking ages, let's go back to the boat," Lara said. She stuffed Dee's small leather bag inside her own backpack before opening the door. Once outside, a shocking sight met their eyes. A stranger was inside the captain's area of their boat. Catching their glances, he started the engine and began to pull the boat away.

"Hey!" cried Tom, Lara, Rufus and Maye together.

They ran along the deck in pursuit as fast as they could. Barney raced ahead of them at an extraordinary pace. He continued the chase until the distance between his body and the boat narrowed and he was running on the ground directly alongside it. As he was just about to leap on board, the powerful engine propelled into top speed and the boat, along with its hijacker, zoomed away into the distance.

Barney flung himself down onto the sandy verge, panting from his colossal effort. Tom, Lara, Rufus and Maye caught up with him and stared into the horizon in dismay. Aaliyah, Dee, Logan and the boat, were gone.

Chapter 25
Akhmim

Barney lifted his head and howled, dismayed that he had not been able to catch the boat thief.

"It's not your fault Barney," said Lara, stroking his head with one hand and pouring water into a dish with another. "You did everything you could. I'm proud of you." Barney lapped up the water then flung himself into Lara's arms, licking her face and neck in appreciation.

"Should we call the police?" asked Tom. "I've got my phone still … but we'd have to ask someone the number here."

"I don't think so." Lara's eyes darted back to the river. "Remember what Aaliyah said about the authorities … there might be some bad guys working there. But we might not have a choice."

"That gang will want Aaliyah to show them the treasure," said Maye, clenching her fists. "Rufus, do you still have the map?"

"No, Aaliyah wanted it back before we arrived here."

"So, the kidnappers will find it in the boat," said Maye with a huff.

"That's good though," said Rufus, his hand on his chin. Everyone stared at him.

"It's not *good*," exclaimed Maye, looking at Rufus as if he had gone mad. "The map's what they wanted."

"But it means we know where they're *going*," Rufus explained. If we follow the same clues without them seeing us, we can rescue Logan, Dee and Aaliyah, capture and tie up the enemies from the gang, then open up the temple and discover the treasure."

"So not *much* we have to do in the next twenty-four hours then," said Lara with a hint of sarcasm. "How are we going to stay hidden, for a start? We don't exactly blend in around here, four kids and a Border collie on their own, roaming around Egypt."

"Well we've got to do *something*," said Tom. "What's the alternative?"

Lara considered for a few moments. They could get in touch with the police, which might lead to trouble. Or she could call her mother on Tom's mobile, but Mrs Jacobs would want them to return home for their own safety and that would mean that Logan, Dee and Aaliyah were on their own.

"You're right," she said with a sigh. "We've got to try."

"How are we going to get to the hospital though?" said Maye. "None of us has money for a taxi."

"I have," said Lara. "We've got Dee's bag, she left it behind with us. Her money and stuff are in there."

"Great," said Rufus. "We should go to the hospital *now* so we can get a head start on the gang. They're probably still looking for the map on the boat."

Forty minutes later, the five were standing in front of a tall, ugly and fairly modern-looking hospital building.

"It doesn't look old enough for an ancient clue to be hidden here," said Rufus, speaking everyone's thoughts. "How will we know where to look?"

"The basement," said Lara. "The ground is the only place here that might be the same as it was. But we need to get in first …"

As she spoke, the automatic doors opened in front of them and a man dressed in a smart shirt and trousers walked out to face them.

"What are you doing here with this dog?" he asked, scowling. "Is somebody sick?"

"Err, no," answered Tom, after a pause.

"Well clear off and find your parents then. Kids and dogs aren't allowed to hang about outside the hospital." He stormed past them and walked around the corner towards the staff car park.

"That's what we have to do then," said Rufus, his eyes creasing as he grinned.

"What, clear off and find our parents?" asked Tom.

"No! One of us has to be *sick*. And let's face it, I'm by far the most talented actor out of us lot, so it should be me."

"And the *humblest*," quipped Lara. "Well, acting does run in your family I suppose," she added, thinking of Rufus' mother in Hollywood who had spent years trying to become an actress.

"Huh! I'm much better than *Mum*. There's a reason all her TV pilots have flopped. Anyway, one person needs to come with me in there. I'll distract them as the rest of you get in."

"It should be you, Maye," said Tom, "in case they only speak Arabic, you'll be the only one who can speak to them."

"But I can't!" Maye looked horrified.

"Why not?" asked Lara. "I thought you wanted to help?"

"Rufus makes me *laugh*," giggled Maye. "If he goes in there, I'll laugh at him. I can't help it."

Lara grabbed Maye's shoulders. "Pull yourself together! This is serious. Logan, Aaliyah and Dee *need* us to rescue them."

"But I don't like Dee much." Maye's smile turned to a frown.

"It doesn't matter," scorned Lara. "They still need us. And you insisted on getting onto that train so you're in this with us now … aren't you?"

"Just take a few deep breaths and think of serious things," suggested Tom. "And whatever you do … don't look at Rufus."

"Okay." Maye stretched her arms and legs as if she were about to start a race. "I'll try."

Maye and Rufus disappeared into the doors as Tom, Lara and Barney waited from outside, hoping the staff would be distracted long enough for them to enter and find the secret entrance.

Chapter 26
The Distraction

Maye walked up to a clean white desk where a young woman was typing at a computer.

"Excuse me," said Maye, her palms sweating. "Erm, my friend ... my friend is sick."

The receptionist looked at the small girl in front of her.

"What's the matter with h—" her eyes were drawn away from Maye to the boy barging through the door. Rufus's entire body was wiggling and shimmying all over the lobby, his skinny legs carrying him from left to right as he barged into the walls.

"I can't ... control ... my body ..." squirmed Rufus. One arm was twisting round and round while he tried to slap it with his other arm and kept missing. "Can't ... stop ..."

Maye fixed her gaze in front of her, away from Rufus, who was now spinning on the floor like a break dancer with his legs kicking in the air.

"Can't … stop …"

The receptionist stared for a few moments, struggling to take in the sight in front of her.

"How long has this been going on for?" she asked.

"About three days," yelled Rufus from the floor.

"Err … well if you could just take a seat … I'll get …"

Rufus got up and moved haphazardly towards the waiting room seats, his arms and legs still flailing wildly. As he pulled a chair out to sit on, he threw it across the room.

"Sorry," he cried, still flinging plastic chairs. "Can't … stop …"

The receptionist looked at Maye.

"I'll need you to fill out some forms for your friend." She placed some papers in front of Maye as Rufus began walking like an ancient Egyptian figure from a painting, pointing his arms and feet. After the receptionist had given Maye a pen, he hurtled towards them both and flung himself over the desk, sending the papers flying. He landed on the other side of the desk next to the receptionist's feet. She screamed in shock and jumped back.

"Sorry, sorry, sorry!" Rufus got up and carried on shimmying, wriggling all the way from his head and shoulders down to his feet. "Can't help it!"

"I'll call for a doctor."

"Here," said Rufus, yanking the desk phone right out of the socket and launching it into the wall. "Oh *darn*. Sorry again!"

The receptionist backed away from the destructive boy and went into the back office to make a phone call.

From outside the building, Tom and Lara had been watching the action through the window. Despite their instructions for Maye, they were both shaking in silent laughter with their sleeves stuffed into their mouths. When the receptionist disappeared into the back room, the pair took their chance and crept through the doors with Barney, past Rufus (who was now swinging from the light fittings) and Maye, through the double doors.

As the doors swung shut, Rufus jumped down and calmly returned all the chairs he had knocked over into an upright position. Maye snuck behind the desk and plugged the phone back into the socket.

The receptionist returned to find the boy and girl standing as still as statues in front of her desk.

"Thanks for all your help," said Rufus. He shook the receptionist's hand as she stared open-mouthed at him.

"I don't know what you did, but I feel right as rain now. Cheerio!"

Rufus and Maye strode out of the building. The receptionist looked at the chairs that were neatly arranged and rubbed her eyes. She spotted the phone back on her desk and picked it up. The dial tone told her it was connected. She dropped the receiver and stared out of the main doors, but Rufus and Maye had gone. Feeling as if she had awoken from a dream, she picked up the phone again and tapped a few numbers.

"No need to come down now, Doctor," she said. "Although I think I've just had another strange daydream …"

Chapter 27
Inside the Hospital

Tom, Lara and Barney found a staircase inside the hospital corridor and hurried down the stairs as far as they could go. The bottom floor of the building was as clean and modern-looking as the rest of the building, with pieces of equipment and files stored.

"It doesn't look like there are any ancient Egyptian tomb openings down *here*," said Tom.

"No, it doesn't …" Lara agreed. "But we should look around anyway." They hunted around, with Barney eagerly joining in, sniffing every corner of the floor. But there was nothing.

"Let's go back up and find Rufus and Maye," said Lara with a sigh.

They climbed the stairs and were about to leave the staircase when a glimpse out of the window stopped Lara in her tracks.

"Look!" she said, pointing outside to an outdoor courtyard in the middle of the hospital building. In the centre of the courtyard was what looked like a miniature temple. It was tiny in comparison to most of the Egyptian temples that Lara had seen in books. *Certainly not a royal temple*, she thought. But the sight was enough to make her heart race.

"That's got to be it," said Tom.

The small structure was circled by red tape and a guard was slumped lazily outside the entrance.

"Looks like we can get to it from over there," said Lara, spotting a patio door leading out to the courtyard from the left of the staircase. She was about to open the door back into the main corridor when Tom pulled her back.

"Wait," he whispered. "Can you hear that?"

They both heard voices coming towards them from the reception area and listened hard.

"You'd better let us go now," said one of the voices. "The British Embassy will be hearing about this!"

"Logan!" Tom and Lara whispered to each other. They crouched behind the door as the footsteps moved past them, then headed back up the stairs to the window. A group of around ten men were making their way into the courtyard, with Logan, Aaliyah and Dee in the middle of the group, each with their hands tied together by their wrists. The man in front of the group pulled a wad of notes from his pocket and handed them to the sleepy guard on duty. After speaking a few words in Arabic, the guard opened the door and most of the group went inside, leaving two men outside as if on watch.

More voices came from the corridor. Barney whimpered as Rufus and Maye walked past the stairway. Lara rushed to open the door and call them back before the two men spotted them from the courtyard. They joined Tom on the staircase looking out into the courtyard.

"It's a good thing we went down to the basement first," whispered Tom. "If we'd paid that guard to let us in, the gang would have found us in there and taken us prisoner as well."

"Barney would have tried to defend us," Lara replied, "but they might have guns." She shuddered at the thought and stroked Barney's head protectively.

A few minutes passed and the five became restless on the staircase.

"Can't we figure out a way to rescue them now?" asked Rufus, who longed for a scheme.

"Too risky," said Tom, "with those guards outside we couldn't even surprise them."

"At least Logan, Dee and Aaliyah look okay," said Lara. "They didn't have any cuts or bruises or anything."

Time continued to drag on.

"I can't *stand* it," cried Rufus, restlessly drumming his hands on the windowsill. "We've got to do something!"

"Shhh," whispered Lara. "They're coming out. Duck!" Everyone dropped their heads down as the group shuffled out of the small building in the courtyard. Voices in Arabic got louder as the group passed the stairway, then became quieter until they faded completely.

"They couldn't find anything," said Maye, who had been listening intently. "They're going to get digging equipment and come back."

"Then we've got to find whatever's there before they come back," said Rufus. "Let's go!"

Chapter 28
The Courtyard

The five entered the courtyard and walked up to the guard. He looked up in surprise. In the ten years he had worked in his relaxed job at the hospital, nobody had ever wanted to go anywhere near the small old building. Now two groups wanted to go inside – and this one had a *dog*. He heaved himself up from his chair and held out his hand. Lara placed a few notes into it.

"More," said the man.

Lara kept going, but the guard said "more" another four times. Feeling impatient, she snatched the notes back from his hand and turned to walk away.

"No, no," cried the man, putting his hand out. "You can go in! Give me back my money!"

Lara gave the money back to the guard and he pulled open the door. The five trooped in and Tom closed the door behind them.

The building was even smaller on the inside than it looked from the outside.

"Those men must have been really cramped in here," said Rufus. "There's hardly room for us."

"And there's nothing *here*," complained Lara. The room contained a stone floor and an opening that looked like a fireplace, but no furniture of any kind. The walls contained faded Egyptian paintings.

Tom tapped the floor.

"It's solid," he said. "I don't think there's a trap door through there."

Rufus crawled into the fireplace. "Nothing here … I can't even see daylight at the top, the chimney's been filled in."

Everyone felt disappointed and wondered what to do next.

"We shouldn't stay here too long," said Tom. "We don't want the gang finding us."

"And that guy outside won't do anything to help us if they come back with another stack of cash," added Rufus.

"Wait," said Lara. "I didn't see a chimney on the outside of this building."

"It's been filled in, I already told you!" Rufus rolled his eyes.

"But even if the chimney got closed … why remove the chimney?" asked Tom.

"Because it's not a fireplace." Lara crawled into the space. "There has to be something up here. Anyone got a torch?"

Tom took a torch from his pocket and flashed it above them. "I can't see anything, but I'm going to take a look." Using his hands and feet he managed to go partly up the small space.

"It gets too small," he said, dropping back down. "I can't reach the top."

"Let me try," said Maye. Tom gave her a leg up and she nimbly climbed upwards. Towards the top, she could just about manage to keep her balance in the narrow space as her feet clung onto the wall on either side.

"There's something up here," she said. "I can pull it with my hands … if I can reach …"

"Go for it, Maye!" yelled Rufus from below.

"Flash more light up here," she called. Tom repointed his torch and Maye got a clearer sight of the lever above her. She strained with her fingers, but it was just out of her reach. Taking a deep breath, she pushed with her feet to propel herself upwards into the space above. Reaching with her hands, she caught the top of the lever, and gravity combined with her own bodyweight moved the lever down sharply.

A rumbling noise groaned next to where Tom, Lara, Rufus and Barney were standing and the floor beneath them began to shake. The stone at the back of what they had thought was a fireplace began to slide downwards, revealing very old and worn steps behind them.

"We did it," Rufus shouted. "A secret entrance!"

Chapter 29
The Opening

Rufus, Lara, Tom and Barney hurried down the first couple of steps until a voice interrupted them.

"Wait! I'm stuck!"

"Oh, sorry Maye," said Tom, stepping back with Lara underneath where the small girl was still dangling from the lever. They joined hands. "Drop down, we'll catch you."

Maye let go and landed awkwardly on top of Tom and Lara as all three fell to the ground. Barney jumped on top on them for good measure and barked excitedly. Unhurt and eager to move on, they re-joined Rufus who was making his way down the secret stairway.

Tom saw another lever on the side on the wall and pulled it. The stone noisily slid back upwards.

"The others are still going to catch up with us at some point if they're coming back with equipment," he said. "They might even have explosives. We need to be careful."

The stairs carried on downwards into the musty passage. Rufus began to sneeze.

"Why do we ... achoo ... end up in ... achoo ... these places."

"It's just dust," said Maye with a giggle.

"I'm a-a-a-choo!"

"He's allergic," said Lara, finishing her cousin's sentence.

"What's allergic? I don't know that word in English."

"It's ... when you have a bad reaction to something," Lara explained.

"A bad reaction?"

"Yeah ... like when you don't get on with something."

"So, I'm allergic to Dee?"

Tom laughed. "No ... well, yeah actually, sort of."

The steps came to an end and the five found themselves in a large space in front of a wall.

"A dead-end?" said Rufus, deflated. "There has to be *something* here."

"Are those drawings on the wall?" said Lara, shining a powerful LED torch from Dee's bag.

"There are three figures," she squinted at the paint that was so faint it almost completely blended into the wall. "And there's something else …"

"A boat," added Tom. "They're standing on a boat."

They moved closer to the wall and examined the pale wall decoration. Rufus tapped the wall and tried feeling for any movement.

"It won't budge," he said, pressing his back into the wall with all his strength. "Maybe if we all—" his eyes fixated on something.

"Maybe if we all what?" asked Lara.

"Look," he answered, pointing above. They all looked up and saw what had grabbed Rufus' attention. High above their heads was a long wooden boat. It appeared to be hanging in the air.

"Wow," Tom marvelled. "Look at that!" He climbed back up the steps and shone his torch to get a better view. "Lara, how old do you think it is?"

I don't know," Lara replied in awe. "But it looks a lot like the boats the ancient Egyptians used to make. I've seen them in my mum's books."

"We've got to get to it," Rufus said. "The boat was on the wall, so it's a clue!"

"I'll climb up there!" Maye tried to scramble up the smooth wall which had no footholds and slipped down twice. Barney ran over to her and barked.

"Stop it Maye," snapped Lara, "you'll break something. Even Barney's telling you to stop."

Maye returned to the others on the steps. "How are we going to get it down?" she asked with her arms folded, still yearning to try to climb up the wall.

"Shame we don't have Logan's backpack with his climbing stuff," said Tom.

"I still don't get how it's up in the air," said Rufus.

"It's resting on stone pillars underneath, see," Tom pointed. "They're coming out of the wall."

"There must be a way to get it down," said Rufus, jumping down from the stairs. "We need to look. Quickly, before the gang finds us."

Everyone searched the space underneath the boat. The floor and walls were bare and smooth, but they were desperate to find something. As the minutes passed, they started to feel worried that the gang would appear coming down the stairs, leaving them with nowhere to hide.

"Can anyone make out anything else in the painting?" called Lara to the others. "There has to be something else here."

Tom and Rufus joined Lara in searching the wall for any part of the drawing that had not faded away. Maye hung back, feeling restless and bored. She took a sip from her bottle of water, then poured some into her hand for Barney who had padded across to sit by her feet. Barney licked the water then tried to grab the bottle from Maye's hand. He had missed playing with his stash of toys during his trip to Egypt and a bottle looked like the next best thing. As Maye stood up, Barney jumped for the bottle again. She began running back and forth with Barney, laughing and shrieking as he chased her around the floor.

"Hey Maye, aren't you going to— ahhh!" While running backwards, Maye had collided straight into Lara and sent water spilling all over both Lara and the wall painting.

"Look!" yelled Rufus, before Lara had time to admonish Maye for soaking her T-shirt. On the wall, where the water had spilt, a new marking appeared. Rufus grabbed Maye's bottle from her hand and sloshed the rest of the water onto the wall.

A number of rectangles appeared on the wall next to the boat, with an 'X' marking the third rectangle from the ground.

"Steps," said Lara, tracing the shape with her fingers. "It's telling us there's something on the third step."

Before Lara had even finished her sentence, Rufus, Tom and Maye had pelted across to the third step. They frantically searched with their hands until Tom felt something on the side.

"I've got it," he yelled. "There's something here that moves." He pushed the side of the step. For two seconds nothing happened, then the steps shot downwards, sending Rufus, Tom and Maye sliding to the ground.

"That didn't help," Rufus complained. "The steps are gone!"

"No," said Lara, pointing to the wall underneath the boat, where steps were now jutting out of the wall. "They're over there."

Chapter 30
The Ancient Boat

"So, the boat wasn't meant to come down," said Rufus, who was beginning to feel as if he were in a computer game rather than real life. "We're going *up*!" He ran across to the steps which were spaced far apart but were not too difficult to climb. The others were not far behind him.

"Barney, stay," commanded Lara, frightened that the dog would slip and fall. He whimpered but obeyed as Lara ascended the steps and pulled herself up into the boat with Maye, Tom and Rufus.

The inside of the boat felt strong and solid; the underground chamber had preserved the ancient wood. Rufus sat by one of four rowing oars. Never being able to resist touching objects, he pulled the oar backwards and a cranking noise echoed from below. Barney barked and ran towards the wall with the painted figures.

"Look," said Tom, leaning over the front of the boat, "part of the wall has lifted!"

Rufus jumped up to see for himself, but as soon as he let go of the oar the wall quickly slammed shut. Barney, caught by surprise, yelped and scratched at the closed wall.

"Let's try the other oars," suggested Lara. The four each took an oar and pulled. The wall once again slid upwards, this time stopping just before reaching the ceiling.

"There's enough space now for us to get through," said Tom, peering over the side of the boat. Their hearts sank as soon as they let go of the oars and heard the wall quickly slide back down again.

"We'll never have time to get there before it shuts," complained Maye.

"What if Lara stays behind?" said Rufus. "Then the rest of us can slide underneath the gap."

"Why does it have to be *me*?" exclaimed Lara, her face twisting with displeasure. "That's just *great*, leave me here to get captured by the enemy while you lot go and discover the treasure! And what about Barney?"

"Oh, he can come with us," said Rufus, with a glint in his eye as Lara's face flushed pink.

"He would *never* leave me here to get captured," stated Lara, folding her arms. Barney woofed in solidarity from below.

"Nobody's staying behind," said Tom. "He's winding you up, Lara."

"Was not." Rufus grinned widely.

"We've already lost three people that we came to Akhmim with," said Tom. "We can't fly the plane home by ourselves … and we can't afford to lose anyone else. There's got to be a way to keep that door open."

"Can we wedge it with something?" suggested Lara. Everyone looked around for an object to use.

"We've only got our bags," said Tom, "and they might just get squashed."

"What if we try and hold it open?" said Rufus.

"Then *we* could get squashed," said Lara. "Which might not be such a bad thing in *your* case."

Rufus stuck out his tongue at his cousin.

"I know what we need to do," stated Maye calmly. Everyone looked at her in surprise. "There's a paddle at the back of the boat. If we pull that at the same time as the oars, the door will open all the way."

Tom, Lara and Rufus spun around to see a large wooden paddle at the back of the boat, stunned that they had completely missed it before. Tom, who had the longest arms and legs of the group, pulled the closest oar with his foot and tried to reach the paddle with his fingers, but the gap was too wide.

"I can't reach," he said with a sigh.

"We need Barney to help," said Rufus.

"No!" shouted Lara. "I don't want him up here, what if he falls? He's worth more to me than *any* treasure."

"He'll be okay, Lara," said Tom softly. "He's got four legs to balance on and if we can get up here, he definitely can. He's already jumped down the Royal Cache, that was really far down."

"Don't remind me!" Lara grimaced.

"We can't do this without Barney," said Rufus. "*And he's an adventurer too, he's part of our team!*"

"Okay," conceded Lara after a pause. "Barney, come! But be careful."

Barney wagged his tail in delight. Within the space of four seconds, he bounded his way up the steps and leapt into the boat.

"Everyone into positions!" yelled Rufus. They each grabbed their oars as Barney watched.

"Barney, grab the paddle!"

"Stick, Barney, stick!"

"Barney, get it!"

Barney tilted his head in confusion. He went to Lara's backpack and pulled out a tennis ball.

"No!" everyone cried at once. "*Paddle!*"

Barney, with the tennis ball in his mouth, slowly cocked his leg up to the side of the boat.

"No!" everyone yelled again, while Rufus laughed so hard that he struggled to keep hold of his oar.

"He thinks ..." he spluttered between chokes of laughter, "he thinks we said *piddle*!"

Maye, Tom and Lara burst into laughter until tears formed in their eyes.

Once she had regained her composure, Lara took the tennis ball from Barney's mouth and hid it back in her bag. She shifted her oar back and forward then pointed back at the paddle. Slowly, Barney turned and looked at the paddle, then looked at Lara, Tom, Rufus and Maye. He placed the top of the paddle in his mouth and walked backwards, pulling it to the side. The door slid open all the way and stopped with a click.

Everyone slowly let go and Barney released the paddle from his mouth. The wall did not move.

"Yesssss!" cried Lara, Rufus, Tom and Maye with cheers and fist pumps. They high fived each other and Barney lifted a paw to high five them each in turn.

Chapter 31
Two Puzzles

The five descended back down the steps and ran through the open wall.

"I can't see a way to close it again," said Tom, looking around for a lever. "That means when the gang arrives, they can walk straight through here."

"We'll have to be quick then," said Rufus, who had already turned the iron handle of a small thick wooden door in front of them.

"Wait!" cried Lara, as Rufus was about to step forward. "Look at the floor, there's a couple of tiles missing."

Behind the door was a perfectly square room with a floor made up of large square tiles. The door led into the corner of the room where the first two tiles in front of the door had given way. Rufus and Lara shone their torches down but could not see the bottom of the dark space below.

"We need to test these tiles before we put all of our weight on them," Lara suggested. "Tom, hold Barney back." Holding onto the doorframe for support, she stamped down with one foot as hard as she could onto the square tile to the right of the door. It crumbled through the ground, leaving another deep space below.

"The whole thing could be a trap," said Maye.

"There has to be a way through," said Rufus, staring at the pattern. "What about the third tile?" Crouching down, he stretched his leg out and kicked down on the tile. It remained intact.

"I think the tiles come in threes," said Lara. "it matches the three people in the boat and the lever on the third step."

Rufus jumped forward onto the step he had just tested.

"This one's safe," he called behind him.

"Well, test the others before you step on them," said Lara. "What are we going to do about Barney? He might put a paw onto one of the other tiles."

"I'll wait till last then carry him," offered Tom.

Lara and Maye followed Rufus across the tiled room. Rufus enjoyed stamping down the false tiles along the way and watching them crash through the floor.

"You're making it easier for the gang to follow the route through now," said Lara.

"Well, if I hadn't, they might have sent Logan, Dee or Aaliyah over the tiles first to test them," he replied. Lara thought that her cousin had a valid point, but did not like to admit it.

At the far end of the room, Rufus opened another identical wooden door and stepped through it with Lara and Maye. They watched as Tom scooped up Barney in his arms and stepped onto the first tile. Barney, who was not used to being carried, started to scramble and wriggle so that Tom, losing his balance, had no choice but to put him down. Barney gleefully bounded from one tile to the next, until he was sitting next to Lara in the doorway.

"We always underestimate you, Barney," said Lara, giving him a pat on the head. "You make me nervous though."

The next room was identical to the previous. After carefully testing each of the tiles, Rufus turned the handle of the next door. It did not open but suddenly sand came pouring into the room from above, showering over the floor.

"Open the door, Rufus!" yelled Lara.

"I *can't*," said Rufus, who was pushing all his weight against the door. "It's jammed!" Tom, Lara and Maye came to help him, but their combined strength was not enough to move the thick door. They ran back to the door they had entered from, which was equally stuck. Sand was quickly filling the room and soon reached their ankles.

"Those things weren't there before," shouted Maye, above the din of the sand storming into the room. Around the edges of the ceiling were masses of small stone figures, each with a bird shaped head and human shoulders. Sand streamed from their mouths.

"It's Horus," said Lara, staring in astonishment. "There were pictures of him at the Temple of Hatshepsut, with his falcon head. He must be protecting the treasure."

"Save us the history lesson," yelled Rufus, trying to kick the sand and dirt away from him, "we need to get out of here!"

"Lara!" yelled Tom. "Give me Barney's tennis ball."

"You want to play a game *now*?" questioned Maye, her eyes wide.

"No, just give it to me, *please!*"

Lara grabbed the ball from her backpack and quickly tossed it to Tom, who took aim and launched the ball up towards one of the falcon heads. It shattered into pieces and the sand stopped spewing from the bird's mouth.

"That's it!" cried Rufus, grabbing the ball from the floor where it had landed. "We've got to get all of them." He threw the ball twice and missed.

"You're as bad as Logan, let Tom do it!" shrieked Lara, staring down at the sand around her calves. Barney sprung across the sand and grabbed the ball where it lay and took it back to Tom, who smashed five more falcons in a row.

"There's too many of them," said Tom, as sand reached his knees. "There must be a hundred!"

Lara grabbed her water bottle and launched it at the Horus statue nearest to her. She hit her target and Barney grabbed the bottle from the floor and brought it back to her. Soon Rufus and Maye joined Tom and Lara in flinging objects from their bags up at the statues as Barney dutifully scrambled around the sand retrieving their belongings.

Finally, Tom struck the final falcon and the sand stopped flowing. Everyone breathed sighs of relief.

Rufus tried the handle of the door again. This time, it opened.

Chapter 32
The Temple of Akhmim

The door opened into the side of a gigantic room, with colossal statues of male and female Egyptian pharaohs guarding both sides of the space. Magnificently preserved paintings lined the walls from top to bottom.

"Wow," Lara gasped, taking in all the sights around her as she shone her torch. Tom took his mobile from his pocket and snapped a few shots.

"Send those to me later," pleaded Rufus, who did not want to miss out on any bragging opportunities with his friends at school.

"Maybe we should light these, so we can see better," said Maye, who had spotted a few old lanterns in the temple.

"We'd better not," Lara replied. "If the gang comes up behind us, we don't want them to know we're here. They'll see the sand and broken tiles, but they won't know that was recent."

"What are we going to do about the gang?" asked Tom, looking behind as if he expected them to emerge immediately through the door. "They'll be here soon after they break through the building in the hospital courtyard and we need to rescue Logan, Dee and Aaliyah."

"Well, first things first," said Rufus. "They're not here yet … and they'll want the treasure, so let's find it before they get here."

The five began to explore the vast temple. The large chamber led into a second, similarly furnished with statues and wall paintings.

"How long do you think it's been since people walked through here?" asked Tom.

"*Thousands* of years," Lara replied. A shiver ran down her spine at the thought.

"There's a whole city above us," said Maye, staring up at the ceiling. "Full of people going to school and work, living their lives." Being in the dark underground temple made Maye, Lara and Tom feel as if they had entered a different age. Lara imagined the priests moving about the chambers in ancient times.

"We need to explore some of these small rooms for gold," said Rufus, bringing everyone back to the present challenge. "All the valuable stuff must have been put somewhere together."

They began investigating some of the side chambers, which apart from more stone statues, did not contain any gold or riches. Finally, an archway brought them into a third large chamber and they found what they had been looking for.

Gold was everywhere: in statues; furniture; sarcophaguses; jewellery and even in piles of coins. Everything gleamed and sparkled against the torchlight.

"Look at all *this*," cried Rufus. "There's even more treasure here than we found in Cornwall in the summer."

"I guess they couldn't fit it all into a side chamber," said Lara, moving around the items but not touching them. "I can't believe we've discovered Egyptian treasure *again*!"

"With help from me," added Maye, hugging her own waist in excitement. "Wait till Karim hears about all *this*."

"We opened the Temple of Akhmim," said Tom to himself, in awe.

"We opened the Temple of *Treasure*," said Rufus.

"Treasure from lots of pharaohs," added Lara. "This is big, no wonder the gang have spent all those years looking for it. But they'll be here soon, and we need a plan."

"Can we plan while eating?" asked Rufus, his stomach growling noisily. "All this tomb-raiding has made me hungry."

They all sat on the floor next to a golden statue of an Egyptian king and pulled out chocolate bars and cakes from their bags. Lara gave Barney some dog treats and poured water into his dish.

"Do you think the gang will know we're here?" asked Tom.

"Well, that guy who stole the boat probably spotted us," said Rufus. "But they don't know we saw the map."

"We'll just have to hope they leave Dee, Logan and Aaliyah somewhere while they're looking for the treasure," said Lara. "Then somehow we've got to trap them down here while we leave and get the authorities."

"We can't trap them in this area," said Maye, "there's no door."

"We'll have to move some of the treasure," suggested Rufus. "If we can move it into one of the small chambers that has a door with bolts, then the gang will think it's all in there and we can lock them in."

"That's assuming they all go into the room at *once*," said Lara. "They might split up, or leave someone to guard their prisoners."

They all paused for a moment, considering whether there were any other options.

"I can't think of anything else," conceded Tom, standing up. "We'll never be able to move these statues, let's move some of the lighter stuff." He grabbed armfuls of jewellery and Lara, Rufus and Maye took his lead. They found a passageway leading from the second main chamber and placed the treasure close enough for the gang to spot as they walked past, but far enough away so that they would have to go inside the corridor before picking it up.

Before they had the chance to go back and fetch more, the sound of voices echoed from the first chamber.

"They're here," Lara whispered.

Chapter 33
The Rescue

Tom, Lara, Rufus, Maye and Barney tiptoed to the tall statues by the edges of the second chamber and hid. Lara held onto Barney's collar to warn him not to growl or make a sound.

The gang moved through the first chamber speaking loudly in Arabic.

"They're looking for the treasure," Maye confirmed. "And it sounds like they're tying up Logan, Aaliyah and Dee by the entrance."

"I'll wait here and try and lock them in the small chamber," said Tom quietly. "When they come through here, you guys sneak into the first chamber and untie the others."

"Let's take off our shoes," suggested Lara, untying her trainers and shoving them into her backpack. "We'll make less sound with our socks." The others followed her lead.

The five waited as the sound of voices and footsteps moved around the first chamber. They all felt stiff with tension and nerves.

"I really hope this works," whispered Rufus under his breath.

The gang members entered the second chamber. Lara, Rufus, Maye and Barney silently slipped back into the first chamber. They saw the group of three prisoners huddled by the entrance next to the sand room, their hands and ankles tied together. Logan looked up and was about to exclaim in surprise when Dee headbutted him sharply.

"Quiet!" she hissed.

Lara, Rufus and Maye quickly got to work untying the ropes. It was extremely difficult to make any progress, as the knots had been fastened so tight.

"Can't you *hurry*?" whispered Dee.

"It's so hard," said Lara, her hands perspiring as she frantically yanked at the knots. It wouldn't be long until the men found the treasure they had left in the small chamber, and Lara, Rufus and Maye felt sick with apprehension in case Tom failed to trap them.

Rufus and Maye managed to untie Logan and Aaliyah's hands at the same time. Logan and Aaliyah started to work on the knots around their ankles as Rufus and Maye turned to help Lara release Dee's hands.

Soon Logan and Aaliyah were free, while everyone was struggling to untie Dee's wrists. Finally, the knots were loosened enough for her to free her hands. But a crashing noise stopped everyone in their tracks.

Tom hurtled towards them from the second chamber with a look of panic on his face.

"I couldn't do it," he gasped. "They're *coming!*"

Chapter 34
The Final Chase

Dee screamed, tugging wildly at the ropes around her ankles. Logan picked her up by the waist and slung her over his shoulder into a fireman's lift. They all raced into the sand room and Tom slammed the door behind them.

"Put me down, you *idiot*," cried Dee. "I'm slowing you down. Leave me!"

"Never!" yelled Logan.

The gang were close behind them as the door to the sand room opened as soon as they had entered the room with the missing tiles. Barney leapt across first, soon followed by Lara, Rufus, Tom, Aaliyah and Maye. Logan was making slower progress as he hopped across the tiles carrying Dee's weight. The door flung open behind them just as Logan took his last step out of the room and slammed the connecting door shut.

"Lara, what are you doing?" yelled Tom, as Lara lingered behind.

"They're catching up with us," she replied. "We need to stop them. Barney – *attack*!"

As the door was yanked open, Barney jumped at the surprised gang member, growling and snapping at his clothes. The man stumbled backwards and almost fell through the missing tiles into the void below.

Lara slammed the door shut again and sped up the passageway with Barney. The others were climbing up a rope that the gang had left to climb down the sloped stairs, Logan still with Dee balanced over his shoulder. Lara stopped in dismay. There was no way she could get Barney up the rope in time before the gang would be at their feet.

Having a sudden brainwave, she pelted to where the third step had been and fumbled her fingers around the side of the slope. Hearing shouts from behind, her heart pounded in her chest as she desperately grasped around. Just as she saw the door to the tiled room open, her fingers pressed on an area that moved. The wall slammed shut from the ceiling, trapping the gang members behind it.

Lara could have cried with relief as the steps next to the boat disappeared back into the wall and the steps leading to their escape route reformed.

"Yeah, Lara!" yelled Rufus from the top of the steps. "We're free!"

Chapter 35
The End of the Adventure

The security guard woke up from his snooze with a start as three adults, four children and a dog trooped out of the ancient building into the courtyard.

"Logan! Put me down *now*," screamed Dee, her face blushing as she flapped her arms over Logan's back. Logan lifted her down onto the ground and untied the knots, releasing her feet. They stared at each other for a few seconds, Logan still panting hard from running and climbing through the temple's entrance with Dee on his back. Dee suddenly flung herself onto Logan, hugging him tightly.

"Thank you," she said with a smile. Logan was too shocked to utter a reply.

"Ewww," yelled Rufus, frowning. "Pack it in!"

Meanwhile, Aaliyah had been speaking to the guard and convinced him to let her use his walkie talkie. A few minutes later the police arrived, and everyone explained what had happened. Dee told how the gang members had found the map in the boat and had kept them as prisoners in case they had been holding back any more clues. Tom, Rufus, Lara and Maye explained how to get the wall open for the police to capture the gang. A team of policemen went down into the underground passage, whilst the others were sent into a police car to be taken to a hotel.

Aaliyah asked to be dropped off at the station.

"Are you sure?" asked Logan. "What if there's a reward for the discovery?"

"I don't want any publicity," said Aaliyah. "I just want to go back to the farm and my family. Thank you … for everything. I've been hiding for too long. Now the gang have been captured, I no longer have to worry."

"It's us who should be thanking you," said Lara. "Without your help, the work my dad started would have been lost forever."

Aaliyah smiled at Lara. "He'd be proud of all of you. I'm sure of it."

After letting Aaliyah out of the car at the station, Lara remembered to give Dee back her bag and belongings. Dee gratefully took them and used her phone to call Clive, her co-pilot.

"Clive's got the plane fixed," she told the others after the call. "Tomorrow we'll get the train back to Cairo, drop Maye off back to her parents and fly back home."

***

As the group ate dinner in the hotel restaurant, Logan's phone started ringing. He looked at it nervously.

"It's your mum," he said, turning to Lara.

Lara swallowed hard.

Logan answered the call and walked away from the table towards the bar. The others watched him as he spoke to Mrs Jacobs, then bent his head down, looking at the floor.

"I bet he's getting torn *apart*," said Rufus, staring with a gruesome level of interest.

"So, will I soon," said Tom. "Your mum's bound to call my mum as soon as she's finished with Logan."

"I hope Mum doesn't take it *all* out on Logan," said Lara, with a pang of guilt. "We all wanted to do this."

"Yeah, he's not a bad guy really, your uncle." Dee looking across at him with a slight smile.

A full thirty minutes passed before Logan returned to the table.

"I've got your mum on speaker," he said to Lara, placing the phone in the middle of the table.

"Hi Mum," said Lara sheepishly.

"Don't 'hi Mum' me," yelled Mrs Jacobs. "You *and* Rufus are grounded as soon as I get back from Egypt."

"You're not coming with us?" asked Lara.

"No … because of your discovery I need to come down from Alexandria and catalogue what's in the temple," replied her mother. "I'm going to call Karim and see if he's got his visa renewed yet so he can come over and help."

"*Yes!*" cried Maye, clapping her hands together in glee. "I'll get to see Karim and tell him all about our adventure."

"Who's that? Karim's sister? Hello there … anyway, Logan will stay with you at home until I get back. *Try* not to go launching yourselves into another dangerous situation."

"But Mum … we found the Temple of Akhmim," said Lara. "We finished what Dad started."

"Yes …" said Mrs Jacobs in a softer tone. "Your dad would have been thrilled by all this … but that *doesn't* mean you're not in a world of trouble for what you've done. I'll be making a list of all the chores you can both do while you're grounded. And I'm going to call Mrs Burt as soon as I finish this call."

Tom groaned and placed his hands on his forehead.

Soon after the call ended, Tom received a call and twenty minutes of scolding from both his mother and father.

"While we're all together still …" started Rufus, "and before we start months of being grounded and doing chores … there's *one thing* left that we need to do." He borrowed Tom's phone and typed *last episode of Logan's Jungle Trek* into YouTube.

"Noooo," cried Logan, covering his hands with his face. "*Seriously?*"

"It is time," said Rufus solemnly.

Logan slumped back in his chair while everyone else leaned in to see the small screen. Barney jumped up into the booth and squeezed next to Lara.

"Here we are on the Amazon river," said Logan in the video, smiling and tweaking his hair while driving a speedboat. "A place where only the strong survive …" He was looking sideways into the camera, oblivious to a large tree branch in the water which he careered the boat straight into. The cameraman jolted backwards but still managed to film Logan falling out of the boat, splashing wildly in the water.

"Gaaaaaaaah!" he yelled. "Something touched my foot!" He splashed and struggled his way over to the river bank where he fell face first into the mud.

"Can we cut this footage, Trev?" he asked, turning to the cameraman.

"This is the live episode," Trevor replied.

A look of panic spread across Logan's features.

"Sooo ..." he said, smearing mud away from his face as he tried to appear professional. "You have to be careful of snakes and creatures in the waters, in this part of the Amazon. But the good thing is, they *don't* tend to appear on the ground."

As Logan spoke a wriggling snake appeared behind him.

"Look behind you," said Trevor, his hand pointing in front of the camera.

"Very funny, Trev," laughed Logan. "As I was saying, in this part of the Amazon ..."

The small snake slid over Logan's feet.

"It's really important to watch your feet and watch where you're— gaaaaaaaah!" Logan screamed down at the snake then turned and pelted through the jungle into the distance. The credits of the video rolled.

Everyone around the table roared with laughter, except Logan who hid his face with his hands.

The next day, after catching the train back to Cairo, the group got into a large taxi and stopped outside Maye's apartment.

"Goodbye," said Maye, her head hanging low as she stood at the bottom of the metal steps.

"We couldn't have done it without you Maye," called Lara from the taxi window. "We'll *never* forget you."

"No, you won't," grinned Maye. She climbed the steps and turned to wave as the car drove off.

***

Two days later, Logan, Rufus, Lara, Tom and Barney were having dinner at a pub in Swindlebrook. It was Tom's last night with his friends before catching the train back to Cornwall the next morning.

"So, when are you taking Dee out on a date?" Lara asked Logan.

"Ewwww!" cried Rufus, screwing his face in disgust. "Lara, I'm *eating* here!"

"My priority is getting a job! I'm hoping your mum will let me stay in Swindlebrook for a while after she gets back." Logan's phone started ringing and Dee's name flashed on the screen. He smiled and blushed as he went to take the call outside.

"Hey, look at this," said Tom, who had been browsing the internet on his phone. "We're in the news. And so is your dad." He handed his phone to Lara and she glanced down at the headline.

Her heart seemed to swell in her chest as she swallowed back tears.

"That's another adventure finished," she said with a watery smile.

"Till the next one!" yelled Rufus, clinking his soda with Lara and Tom and patting Barney on the head. "Cheers!"

Acknowledgements

While a writer spends most of their time working alone, there are so many people who have helped me in my writing to date that I would not have been able to publish a single book without them, let alone two!

Thank you to all my family, especially to my mum (Dawn), and brother (Jeff), for being there for me through everything.

Thank you to all my friends who have shown so much enthusiasm for my writing, including Emma, Emma and Emma (yes, most the people I know are called Emma); Holly; Helly; Matt; Craig; Jeffrey; Rhiannon; Emily; Abi and every single person who has reached out to me from both sides of the pond and beyond since the start of my writing journey. It really means a lot to me.

Thank you to the dream team of professionals who have helped turn *The Adventurers 1 and 2* into the best books that they can be. To Andrew whose beautiful cover art brings the stories to life in a spectacular way. To Amanda at Let's Get Booked, editor extraordinaire, for spotting so many things that I miss. And to Bojan for neatly formatting my words onto pages and screens.

Last and certainly not least, thank you to every single reader. Thank you for sharing in Lara, Tom, Rufus and Barney's adventures, and for making it possible for me to live mine!

About the Author

Photo by Emily Dews Photography

Jemma Hatt grew up near Sevenoaks in Kent where she developed a passion for reading and writing short stories, which ultimately led to a degree in English Literature from the University of Exeter.

The Adventurers Series was inspired by many family holidays to Devon and Cornwall, as well as the adventure stories she loved reading as a child. After having lived and worked in London, New York and Delaware, Jemma is now based in Kent and working on the next Adventurers stories as well as other writing projects.

Stay up-to-date with Jemma's writing and access free giveaways and offers by signing up to her newsletter at www.jemmahatt.com (if you are under 13 please ask an adult to sign up for you).

THE ADVENTURERS AND THE CURSED CASTLE

By Jemma Hatt

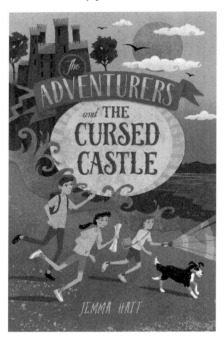

A mysterious curse has stricken Kexley Castle for generations ever since Egyptian treasure was transported to Cornwall by a 19th Century explorer. Can four young adventurers reveal the secrets that have been hidden for over a hundred years?

THE ADVENTURERS AND THE CITY OF SECRETS

By Jemma Hatt

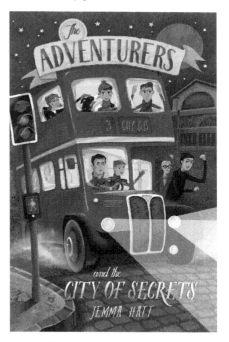

Two master criminals are on the run with ancient treasure, using London's web of hidden trails and passages to conceal their loot. The Adventurers must track them down using their wits, Uncle Logan ... and a stolen red bus.

Join Lara, Rufus, Tom, Daisy and Barney as they race to uncover the City of Secrets!

THE ADVENTURERS AND THE CONTINENTAL CHASE

By Jemma Hatt

JEMMA HATT

A kidnap in Paris … a chase across Europe …

one epic road trip!

The Adventurers are on holiday when Maye warns of suspicious activity in Paris. Join them as they race from the French Alps to the ancient ruins of Rome on the trail of a dangerous gang with a legacy of secrets.

THE ADVENTURERS AND THE JUNGLE OF JEOPARDY

By Jemma Hatt

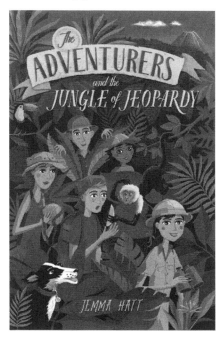

A TV show has turned into a dangerous game... can six young challengers succeed against the odds?

Join Lara, Rufus and the gang on their most perilous adventure yet. The race is on to discover Teo's treasure, but the jungle has obstacles to overcome!

Printed in Great Britain
by Amazon

73370366R00116